THE
R.A. LAFFERTY
FANTASTIC
MEGAPACK®

THE
R.A. LAFFERTY
FANTASTIC
MEGAPACK®

R.A. LAFFERTY

WILDSIDE PRESS

* * * *

"Introduction" is copyright © 2016 by Wildside Press LLC.

"Aloys" was originally published in *Galaxy Magazine*, August 1961.

"Adam Had Three Brothers" was originally published in *New Mexico Quarterly Review*, Fall 1960.

"Seven-Day Terror" was originally published in *If*, March 1962.

"Day of the Glacier" was originally published in *Science Fiction Stories*, January 1960.

"Sodom and Gomorrah, Texas" was originally published in *Galaxy Magazine*, December 1962.

"Through Other Eyes " was originally published in *Future Science Fiction*, No. 47, February 1960.

"The Weirdest World" was originally published in *Galaxy Magazine*, June 1961.

"The Six Fingers Of Time," by R. A. Lafferty" was originally published in *If*, September 1960.

"Try to Remember" was originally published in *Collage Magazine*, December 1960/January 1961.

"McGonigal's Worm" was originally published in *If*, November 1960.

"*The Polite People of Pudibundia*" was originally published in If, January 1961.

"In the Garden" was originally published in *If*, March 1961.

"All the People" was originally published in *Galaxy Magazine*, April 1961.

"Dream" was originally published in *Galaxy Magazine*, June 1962.

"The Wagons" was originally published in *New Mexico Quarterly Review*, Spring 1959.

"Other Side of the Moon" was originally published in *Husk Magazine*, March 1960.

"The Ugly Sea" was originally published in *The Literary Review*, Fall 1960.

"Saturday You Die" was originally published in *Artesian Magazine*, Spring 1960.

CONTENTS

INTRODUCTION

Raphael Aloysius Lafferty was born on November 7, 1914, in Neola, Iowa to Hugh David Lafferty, a broker dealing in oil leases and royalties, and Julia Mary Burke, a teacher. He was the youngest of five siblings. His first name, Raphael, derived from the day on which he was expected to be born—the Feast of St. Raphael.

When Ray (as he was called) was 4 years old, his family moved to Perry, Oklahoma. He graduated from Cascia Halland later attended night school at the University of Tulsa for two years starting in 1933, mostly studying math and German, but left before graduating. He then began to work for a Clark Electric Co. in Tulsa, Oklahoma, and apparently a newspaper as well; during this period (1939–1942), he attended the International Correspondence School.

Lafferty lived most of his life in Tulsa, with his sister, Anna Lafferty. Lafferty enlisted in the U.S. Army in 1942. After training in Texas, North Carolina, Florida, and California, he was sent to the South Pacific Area, serving in Australia, New Guinea, Morotai and the Philippines. When he left the Army in 1946, he had become a 1st Sergeant serving as a staff sergeant and had received an Asiatic-Pacific Campaign Medal. He never married.

He did not begin writing until the 1950s, but he wrote thirty-two novels and more than 200 short stories, most of them at least nominally science fiction. His first published story (included here) was "The Wagons" in *New Mexico Quarterly Review* in 1959. His first published science fiction story was "Day of the Glacier" (also included here) in *The Original Science Fiction Stories* in 1960, and his first published novel was *Past Master* (1968).

Until 1971, Lafferty worked as an electrical engineer. After that, he spent his time writing until around 1980, when his output declined due to a stroke. He stopped writing regularly in 1984. In 1994, he suffered an even more severe stroke. He died 18 March 2002, aged 87 in a nursing home in Broken Arrow, Oklahoma. His collected papers, artifacts, and ephemera were donated to the University of Tulsa's McFarlin Library, Department of Special Collections and University Archives. Other manuscripts are housed in the University of Iowa's Library special collections department.

Lafferty's funeral took place at Christ the King Catholic Church in Tulsa, where he regularly attended daily Mass. He is buried at St. Rose Catholic Cemetery in Perry

Without a doubt, he was one of the most quirky and unusual authors every to work in science fiction. I only met him once, at a World Science Fiction Convention (we were on a panel together, along with Jack Chalker and several others). He was a quiet but knowledgable on the subject—small press publishing—because small presses had long championed his work. For many years, Wildside Press was his primary publisher.

Enjoy!

—John Gregory Betancourt
Publisher, Wildside Press LLC

ALOYS

He had flared up more brightly than anyone in memory. And then he was gone. Yet there was ironic laughter where he had been; and his ghost still walked. That was the oddest thing: to encounter his ghost.

It was like coming suddenly on Haley's Comet drinking beer at the Plugged Nickel Bar, and having it deny that it was a celestial phenomenon at all, that it had ever been beyond the sun. For he could have been the man of the century, and now it was not even known if he was alive. And if he were alive, it would be very odd if he would be hanging around places like the Plugged Nickel Bar.

This all begins with the award. But before that it begins with the man.

Professor Aloys Foulcault-Oeg was acutely embarrassed and in a state of dread.

"These I have to speak to, all these great men. Is even glory worth the price when it must be paid in such coin?"

Aloys did not have the amenities, the polish, the tact. A child of penury, he had all his life eaten bread that was part sawdust, and worn shoes that were part cardboard. He had an overcoat that had been his father's, and before that his grandfather's.

This coat was no longer handsome, its holes being stuffed and quilted with ancient rags. It was long past its years of greatness, and even when Aloys had inherited it as a young man it was in the afternoon of its life. And yet it was worth more than anything else he owned in the world.

Professor Aloys had become great in spite of—or because of?—his poverty. He had worked out his finest theory, a series of nineteen interlocked equations of cosmic shapeliness and simplicity. He had worked it out on a great piece of butchers' paper soaked with lamb's blood, and had so given it to the world.

And once it was given, it was almost as though nothing else could be added on any subject whatsoever. Any further detailing would be only footnotes to it and all the sciences no more than commentaries.

Naturally this made him famous. But the beauty of it was that it made him famous, not to the commonalty of mankind (this would have been a burden to his sensitively tuned soul), but to a small and scattered class of extremely erudite men (about a score of them in the world). Their recognition brought him almost, if not quite, complete satisfaction.

But he was not famous in his own street or his own quarter of town. And it was in this stark conglomerate of dark-souled alleys and roofs that Professor Aloys had lived all his life till just thirty-seven days ago.

When he received the announcement, award, and invitation, he quickly calculated the time. It was not very long to allow travel halfway around the world. Being locked out of his rooms, as he often was, he was unencumbered by baggage or furniture, and he left for the ceremony at once.

With the announcement, award, and invitation, there had also been a check; but as he was not overly familiar with the world of finance or with the English language in which it was written, he did not recognize it for what it was. Having used the back of it to write down a formula that had crept into his mind, he shoved the check, forgotten, into one of the pockets of his greatcoat.

* * * *

For three days he rode a river boat to the port city, hidden and hungry. There he concealed himself on an ocean tramp. That he did not starve on this was due to the caprice of the low-lifers who discovered him, for they made him stay hidden in a terrible bunker and every day or two they passed in a bucket to him.

Then, several ports and many days later, he left the ship like a crippled, dirty animal. And it was in That City and on That Day. For the award was to be that evening.

"These I have to speak to, all these wonderful men who are higher than the grocers, higher than the butchers even. These men get more respect than a policeman, than a canal boat captain. They are wiser than a mayor and more honored than a merchant. They know arts more intricate than a clock-maker's and are virtuous beyond the politicians. More perspicacious than editors, more talented than actors, these are the great men of the world. And I am only Aloys, and now I am too ragged and dirty even to be Aloys any more. I no longer am a man with a name."

For he was very humble as he walked the great town where even the shop girls were dressed like princesses, and all the restaurants were so fine that only the rich people would have dared to go in them at all. Had there been poor people (and there were none) there would have been no place for them to eat.

"But it is to me they have given the prize. Not to Schellendore and not to Ottlebaum, not to Francks nor Timiryaseff, not even to Pitirim-Koss, the latchet of whose shoe I am not—but why do I say that?—he was not, after all, very bright—all of them are inadequate in some way—the only one who was ever able to get to the heart of these great things was Aloys

Foulcault-Oeg, who happens to be myself. It is a strange thing that they should honor me, and yet I believe they could not have made a better choice."

So pride and fear warred in him, but it was always the pride that lost. For he had only a little bit of pride, undernourished and on quaking ground, and against it was a whole legion of fears, apprehensions, shames, dreads, embarrassments, and nightmarish bashfulnesses.

He begged a little bit when he had found a poor part of town. But even here the people were of the rich poor, not the poor as he had known them.

When he had money in his pocket, he had a meal. Then he went to Jiffy Quick While You Wait Cleaners Open Day and Night to have his clothes cleaned. He wrapped himself in dignity and a blanket while he waited. And as the daylight was coming to an end, they brought his clothes back to him.

"We have done all we could do. If we had a week or a month, we might do a little more, but not much."

* * * *

Then he went out into the town, cleaner than he had been in many years, and he walked to the hall of the Commendation and Award. Here he watched all the great men arrive in private cars and taxis: Ergodic Eimer, August Angstrom, Vladimir Vor. He watched them and thought of what he would say to them, and then he realized that he had forgotten his English.

"I remember dog, that is the first word I ever learned, but what will I say to them about a dog? I remember house and horse and apple and fish. Oh, now I remember the entire language. But what if I forget it again? Would it not be an odd speech if I could only say apple and fish and house and dog? I would be shamed."

He wished he were rich and could dress in white like the street sweepers, or in black leather like the newsboy on the corner. He saw Edward Edelstein and Christopher Cronin enter and he cowered on the street and knew that he would never be able to talk to those great men.

A fine gentleman came out and walked directly to him.

"You are the great Professor Foulcault-Oeg? I would have known you anywhere. True greatness shines from you. Our city is honored tonight. Come inside and we will go to a little room apart, for I see that you will have to compose yourself first. I am Graf-Doktor Hercule Bienville-Stravroguine."

Whyever he said he was the Graf-Doktor is a mystery, because he was Willy McGilly and the other was just a name that he made up that minute.

Within, they went to a small room behind the cloak room. But here, in spite of the smooth kindness of the gracious gentleman, Aloys knew that he would never be able to compose himself. He was an epouvantail, a pugalo, a clown, a ragamuffin. He looked at the nineteen-point outline of the address he was to give. He shuddered and he gobbled like a turkey. He sniffled and he wiped his nose on his sleeve. He was terrified that the climax of his life's work should find him too craven to accept it. And he discovered that he had forgotten his English again.

"I remember bread and butter, but I don't know which one goes on top. I know pencil and pen-knife and bed, but I have entirely forgotten the word for maternal uncle. I remember plow, but what in the world will I say to all these great men about a plow? I pray that this cup may pass from me."

Then he disintegrated in one abject mass of terror. Several minutes went by.

* * * *

But when he emerged from the room he was a different man entirely. Erect, alive, intense, queerly handsome, and now in formal attire, he mounted with the sure grace of a panther to the speaker's platform. Once only he glanced at the nineteen-point outline of his address. As there is no point in keeping it a secret, it was as follows: 1. Cepheid and Cerium— How Long Is a Yardstick? 2. Double Trouble—Is Ours a Binary Universe? 3. Cerebrum and Cortex—the Mathematics of Melancholia. 4. Microphysics and Megacyclic Polyneums. 5. *Ego, No, Hemeis*—the Personality of the Subconscious. 6. Linear Convexity and Lateral Intransigence. 7. Betelgeuse Betrayed—the Myth of Magnitude. 8. Mu-Meson, the Secret of Metamorphosis. 9. Theogony and Tremor—the Mathematics of Seismology. 10. Planck's Constant and Agnesi's Variable. 11. Dien-cephalon and Di-Gamma—Unconscionable Thoughts about Consciousness. 12. Inverse Squares and the Quintesimal Radicals. 13. The Chain of Error in the Lineal B Translation. 14. Skepticism—the Humor of the Humorless. 15. Ogive and Volute—Thoughts on Celestial Curviture. 16. Conic Sections—Small Pieces of Infinity. 17. Eschatology—Medium Thoughts about the End. 18. Hypo-polarity and Cosmic Hysteresis. 19. The Invisible Quadratic, or This is All Simpler than You Think.

You will immediately see the beauty of this skeleton, and yet to flesh it would not be the work of an ordinary man.

He glanced over it with the sure smile of complete confidence. Then he spoke softly to the master of ceremonies in a whisper with a rumble that could be heard throughout the hall.

"I am here. I will begin. There is no need for any further introduction."

For the next three and a half hours he held that intelligent audience completely spellbound, enchanted. They followed, or seemed to follow, his lightning flashes of metaphor illumining the craggy chasms of his vasty subjects.

They thrilled to the magnetic power of his voice, urbane yet untamed, with its polyglot phrasing and its bare touch of accent so strange as to be baffling; ancient, surely, and yet from a land beyond the Pale. And they quivered with interior pleasure at the glorious unfolding in climax after climax of these before only half-glimpsed vistas.

Here was a world of mystery revealed in all its wildness, and it obeyed and stood still, and he named its name. The nebula and the conch lay down together, and the ultra-galaxies equated themselves with the zeta mesons. Like a rich householder, he brought from his store treasures old and new, and nothing like them had ever been seen or heard before.

* * * *

At one point Professor Timiryaseff cried out in bafflement and incomprehension, and Doctor Ergodic Eimer buried his face in his hands, for even these most erudite men could not glimpse all the shattering profundity revealed by the fantastic speaker.

And when it was over they were limp and delighted that so much had been made known to them. They had the crown without the cross, and the odd little genius had filled them with a rich glow.

The rest was perfunctory, commendations and testimonials from all the great men. The trophy, heavy and rich but not flashy, worth the lifetime salary of a professor of mathematics, was accepted almost carelessly. And then the cup was passed quietly, which is to say the tall cool glasses went around as the men still lingered and talked with hushed pleasure.

"Gin," said the astonishing orator. "It is the drink of bums and impoverished scholars, and I am both. Yes, anything at all with it."

Then he spoke to Maecenas, who was at his side, the patron who was footing the bill for all this gracious extravagance.

"The check I have never cashed, having been much in movement since I have received it. And as to me it is a large amount, though perhaps not to others, and as you yourself have signed it, I wonder if you could cash it for me now."

"At once," said Maecenas, "at once. Ten minutes and we shall have the sum here. Ah, you have endorsed it with a formula! Who but Professor Aloys Foulcault-Oeg could be so droll? Look, he has endorsed it with a formula!"

"Look, look! Let us copy! Why, this is marvelous! It takes us even beyond his great speech of tonight. The implications of it!"

"Oh, the implications!" they said as they copied it off, and the implications rang in their heads like bells of the future.

Now it had suddenly become very late, and the elated little man with the gold and gemmed trophy under one arm and the packet of bank notes in his pocket disappeared as by magic.

* * * *

Professor Aloys Foulcault-Oeg was not seen again; or, if seen, he was not known, for hardly anyone would have known his face. In fact, when he had painfully released the bonds by which he had been tied in the little room behind the cloak room, and removed the shackles from his ankles, he did not pause at all, but slipped into his greatcoat and ran out into the night. Not for many blocks did he even remove the gag from his mouth, not realizing in his confusion what it was that obstructed his speech and breathing. But when he got it out, it was a pleasant relief.

A kind gentleman took him in hand, the second to do so that night. He was bundled into a kind of taxi and driven to a mysterious quarter called Wreckville. And deep inside a secret building he was given a bath and a bowl of hot soup. And later he gathered with others at a festive board.

Here Willy McGilly was king. As he worked his way into his cups with the gold trophy in front of him, he expounded and elucidated.

"I was wonderful. I held them in the palm of my hand. Was I not wonderful, Oeg?"

"I could not hear all, for I was on the floor of the little room. But from what I could hear, yes, you were wonderful."

"Only once in my life did I give a better speech. It was the same speech, but it was newer then. This was in Little Dogie, New Mexico, and I was selling a snake-oil derivative whose secret I still cannot reveal. But I was good tonight and some of them cried. And now what will you do, Oeg? Do you know what we are?"

"*Moshennekov.*"

"Why, so we are."

"*Schwindlern.*"

"The very word."

"Low-life con men. And the world you live on is not the one you were born on. I will join you if I may."

"Oeg, you have a talent for going to the core of the apple."

For when a man (however unlikely a man) shows real talent, then the Wreckville bunch has to recruit him. They cannot have uncontrolled talent running loose in the commonalty of mankind.

ADAM HAD THREE BROTHERS

In the town there are many races living, each in its own enclave, some of many square miles, some of a few acres only, some of but one or two streets. Its geographers say that it has more Italians than Rome, more Irish than Dublin, more Jews than Israel, more Armenians than Yerevan.

But this overlooks the most important race of all.

There is the further fact (known only to the more intense geographers): it has more Rrequesenians than any town in the world. There are more than a hundred of them.

By the vulgar the Rrequesenians are called Wrecks, and their quarter is Wreckville. And there is this that can be said of them that cannot be said of any other race on earth: Every one of them is a genius.

These people are unique. They are not Gypsies, though they are often taken for them. They are not Semites. They are not even children of Adam.

* * * *

Willy McGilley, the oldest of the Wrecks (they now use Gentile names) has an old baked tablet made of straw and pressed sheep dung that is eight thousand years old and gives the true story of their origin. Adam had three brothers: Etienne, Yancy, and Rreq. Etienne and Yancy were bachelors. Rreq had a small family and all his issue have had small families; until now there are about two hundred of them in all, the most who have ever been in the world at one time. They have never intermarried with the children of Adam except once. And not being of the same recension they are not under the same curse to work for a living.

So they do not.

Instead they batten on the children of Adam by clever devices that are known in police court as swindles.

Catherine O'Conneley by ordinary standards would be reckoned as the most beautiful of the Wrecks. By at least three dozen men she was considered the most beautiful girl in the world. But by Wreckian standards she was plain. Her nose was too small, only a little larger than that of ordinary women; and she was skinny as a crow, being on the slight side of a hundred and sixty. Being beautiful only by worldly standards she was reduced even more than the rest of them to living by her wits and charms.

She was a show girl and a bar girl. She gave piano lessons and drawing lessons and tap-dancing lessons. She told fortunes and sold oriental rugs and junk jewelry, and kept company with lonely old rich men. She was able to do all these things because she was one bundle of energy.

She had no family except a number of unmarried uncles, the six Petapolis brothers, the three Petersens, the five Calderons, the four Oskamans; and Charley O'Malley, nineteen in all.

* * * *

Now it was early morning and a lady knocked at her door.

"The oil stock is no good. I checked and the place would be three hundred miles out to sea and three miles down. My brother says I've been took."

"Possibly your brother isn't up on the latest developments in offshore drilling. We have the richest undeveloped field in the world and virtually no competition. I can promise we will have any number of gushers within a week. And if your brother has any money I can still let him have stock till noon today at a hundred and seventy-five dollars a share."

"But I only paid twenty-five a share for mine."

"See how fast it has gone up in only two days. What other stock rises so fast?"

"Well all right, I'll go tell him."

* * * *

There was another knock on the door.

"My little girl take piano lessons for six weeks and all she can play is da da da."

"Good. It is better to learn one note thoroughly than just a little bit of all of them. She is not ready for the other notes yet. But I can tell you this: she is the most intelligent little girl I have ever seen in my life and I believe she has a positive genius for the piano. I truly believe she will blossom all at once and one of these days she will be playing complete symphonies."

"You really think so?"

"I do indeed."

"Well then I will pay you for six more weeks, but I do wish she could play more than da da da."

* * * *

There was another knock at the door.

"Honey Bun, there was something wrong. I give you ten dollars to bet on Summertime in the first race at Marine Park; you say it's a sure thing and fifty to one. But now I find there isn't any such track as Marine Park and nobody ever heard of the horse. Huh, Honey Bun? What you do to your best boy friend?"

"O, we use code names. What if all these hot tips ever got out? Summertime of course was Long Day and Marine Park was Jamaica. And he only lost by about six noses. Wasn't that good for a fifty to one? And now I have an even better tip. It's so hot I can't even tell you the name of the horse, but I feel sure that twenty would get you a thousand."

"All the time I give you money but never I win yet, Honey Bun. Now you give a little kiss and we talk about another bet."

"I had surely thought our attachment was on a higher plane."

"Words, Honey Bun, always words. But you give, um, um, um, that's good. Now I bet again, but I bet I better win someday."

* * * *

There was another knock on the door.

"How come you let my brother-in-law in on a good thing and never tell me? For a hundred he'll have two hundred and fifty in a week, and you never tell me, and I'm your friend and never persecute you when you don't pay your bill."

So she had to give her caller the same deal she had given his brother-in-law.

* * * *

After that she went out to take the game out of her traps. She had set and baited them some days before. She had gone to see five hundred people, which took quite a while even for one with her excess of energy. And to each she said this:

"I have just discovered that I have an infallible gift of picking winners. Now I want you to give it a test. Here is a sure winner I have picked. I ask you bet it, not with me, not with one of my uncles, but with a bookie of your own choice. I prefer not to know with whom you bet."

Of the five hundred there were a hundred and forty-four winners, very good. So the next day she went to the hundred and forty-four with even more assurance and offered them the same proposition again. And of the hundred and forty-four there were fifty-six winners. Very good, for she really could pick them.

To these fifty-six she went the third day and offered them the third sure bet free. And incredibly of the fifty-six there were nineteen winners.

This was repeated the next day, and of the nineteen there were seven winners.

Now she went to talk money. The seven lucky clients could not deny that she indeed had the gift of picking winners. She had given them all four straight in four days and her secret should surely be worth money. Besides, they had all let their bets ride and they had won a lot, an average of more than six hundred dollars.

But she would give no more free tips. She would only sell her complete and exclusive secret for a thousand dollars. And she collected from six of them. The seventh was Mazuma O'Shaunessey.

"I have given you four straight winners, but I cannot give you any more free tips. We will now talk cold turkey."

"O, put it in a basket, Katie."

"Why, what do you mean, sir?"

"I learned it in my cradle. The Inverted Pyramid. You tapped five hundred, and you got besides me how many? Five?"

"Six besides you, seven in all."

"Very good. You pick them nice for a little girl. But isn't that a lot of work for no more than a hatful of money?"

"Six thousand dollars is a large hatful. And there is always one smart alec like you who knows it all."

"Now Kate dear, let's look at it this way. I can really pick all the winners, not seven straights in five hundred, but all five hundred if I wished."

"O hah, you can't fool this little-goose."

"O, I could prove it easily enough, but that's showy and I hate to be a show-off. So I suggest that you take my word for it and share my secret with me and give up this penny ante stuff."

"And all you want for your sure thing secret is five thousand dollars or so?"

"Why Kate, I don't want your money. I have so much that it's a burden to me. I only want to marry you."

* * * *

She looked at him and she was not sure. O, not about marrying him, he was nice enough. She was not sure, she had never been sure, that he was a Wreck.

"Are you?"

"Why Kate, does one Wreck have to ask another that question?"

"I guess not. I'll go ask my uncles what they think. This is something of a decision."

She went to see all her bachelor uncles and asked them what they knew about Mazuma O'Shaunessey.

He was known to all of them.

"He is a competent boy, Kate," said Demetrio Petapolis. "If I do not miscount I once came out a little short on a deal with him. He knows the Virginia City Version, he knows the old Seven-Three-Three, he can do the

Professor and His Dog, and the Little Audrey. And he seems to be quite rich. But is he?"

He meant, not is he rich, but—is he a Wreck?

"Does one Wreck have to ask another that question?" said Kate.

"No, I guess not."

* * * *

Hodl Oskanian knew him too.

"That boy is real cute. It seems in the last deal I had with him he came out a little ahead. It seems that in every deal I have with him he comes out a little ahead. He knows the Denver Deal and the Chicago Cut. He does the Little Old Lady and the Blue Hat. He knows the Silver Lining and the Doghouse and the Double Doghouse. And he seems quite likeable. But is he?"

He meant, not was he likeable, but—was he a Wreck?

"Cannot one Wreck always tell another?" said Kate loftily.

* * * *

Lars Petersen knew Mazuma too.

"He is a klog pog. He knows the Oslo Puds and the Copenhagen Streg. He knows the Farmer's Wife and the Little Black Dog. He can do the Seventy-Three and the Supper Club. And he runs more tricks with the Sleepy River than anyone I ever saw, and has three different versions of the Raft and four of Down the Smoke Stack. And all the officers on the bilk squad give him half their pay every week to invest for them. He seems quite smart. But is he?"

He meant, not was he smart, but—is he a Wreck?

"Should one have to ask?" said Kate haughtily.

* * * *

Her uncle Charley O'Malley also thought well of Mazuma. "I am not sure but that at last count he was a raol or so ahead of me. He knows the Blue Eyed Drover and the Black Cow. He can do the Brandy Snifter with the best of them, and he isn't bashful with the Snake Doctor. He does a neat variation of the Bottom of the Barrel. He can work the Yellow Glove and the Glastonburry Giveaway. And he seems affable and urbane. But is he?"

He meant, not was he affable and urbane (he was), but—is he a Wreck? Ah, that was the question.

"How can you even ask?" said Kate.

* * * *

So they were married and began one of the famous love affairs of the century. It went on for four years and each day brought new high adventure.

They purged for the good of his soul a Dayton industrialist of an excessive sum of cash and thus restored his proper sense of values and taught him that money isn't everything. They toured the world in gracious fashion and took no more than their ample due for their comfortable maintenance. They relaxed the grip of tight-fisted Frenchmen and retaught them the stern virtues of poverty. They enforced an austere regime of abstinence and hard work on heretofore over-wealthy and over-weight German burghers and possibly restored their health and prolonged their lives. They had special stainless steel buckets made to bury their money in, and these they scattered in many countries and several continents. And they had as much fun as it is allowed mortals to have.

One pleasant afternoon Mazuma O'Shaunessey was in jail in a little town in Scotland. The jailer was gloomy and suspicious and not given to joking.

"No tricks from you now. I will not be taken."

"Just one to show I have the power. Stand back so I can't reach you."

"I'm not likely to let you."

"And hold up a pound note in one hand as tightly as you can. I will only flick my handkerchief and the note will be in my hand and no longer in yours."

"Man I defy you. You cannot do it."

He held the note very tightly and closed his eyes with the effort. Mazuma flicked his handkerchief, but the Scotsman was right. He could not do it. This was the only time that Mazuma ever failed. Though the world quivered on its axis (and it did) yet the note was held so tightly that no power could dislodge it. But when the world quivered on its axis the effect was that Mazuma was now standing outside the cell and the Scotsman was within. And when the Chief came some minutes later Mazuma was gone and the Scotch jailer stood locked in the cell, his eyes still closed and the pound note yet held aloft in a grip of steel. So he was fired, or cashiered as the Old Worlders call it, for taking a bribe and letting a prisoner escape. And this is what usually comes as punishment to overly suspicious persons.

* * * *

Katie still used the Inverted Pyramid and very effectively. Mazuma did not really have an unfailing talent for picking winners. He'd only said that to get Kate to marry him, and it was the best lie he ever told. But he did have an infallible talent for many things, and they thrived.

The first little cloud in the sky came once when they passed a plowman in a field in the fat land of Belgium.

"Ah, there is a happy man," said Mazuma. "Happy at work."

"Happy at work? O my God, what did you say? What kind of words are these, my husband?"

But in the months and years that followed, this frightening incident was forgotten.

The couple became the pride of Wreckville when they returned as they did several times a year and told their stories. Like the time the state troopers ran them down and cornered them with drawn guns.

"O, we don't want to take you in. We'll report that we couldn't catch you. Only tell us how you do it. We don't want to be troopers all our lives."

And the time they ran a little house in Faro Town itself. It was a small upstairs place and Katie played the piano, and they had only one bartender, a faded little blonde girl with a cast in one eye, and only one table where Mazuma presided. And this where all the other Casinos were palaces that would make Buckingham look like a chicken coop.

And the funny thing is that they took in no money at all. The barmaid would always say all drinks were ten dollars, or failing that they were on the house; as they used no coin and had trays in the register for only tens, fifties, hundreds and thousands. It was too much trouble to do business any other way.

Katie would bait her money jar with several hundred dollar bills and one or two larger, and demurely refuse anything smaller for selections as she didn't want the jar filled up with wrapping paper. So she would tinkle along all night and all drinks were on the house, which was not too many as only three could sit at the bar at once.

And Mazuma never shook or dealt a game. He had only blue chips as he said any other color hurt his eyes. And no matter what the price of the chips, it was legendary and gained zeros as it was retold.

Several of the larger sports came up the stairs out of curiosity. And their feelings were hurt when they were told they were too little to play, for they weren't little at all. So Mazuma sat all night Monday through Friday and never cut a hand or shook a bone.

Then on Saturday night the really big boys came upstairs to see what it was about. They were the owners of the nine big Casinos in town, and six of these gentlemen had to sit on boxes. Their aggregate worth would total out a dollar and thirteen cents to every inhabitant of the U.S.

Katie tinkled tunes all night for a hundred to five hundred dollars a selection, and Mazuma dealt on the little table. And when the sun came up they owned a share of all nine of the big Casinos, and had acquired other assets besides.

Of course these stories of Katie and Mazuma were topped, as about half the Wrecks went on the road, and they had some fancy narrations when they got back to Wreckville.

* * * *

And then the bottom fell out of the world.

They had three beautiful children now. The oldest was three years old and he could already shake, deal, shuffle, and con with the best of them. He knew the Golden Gambit and the Four Quarters and the Nine Dollar Dog and Three Fish Out. And every evening he came in with a marble bag full of half dollars and quarters that he had taken from the children in the neighborhood. The middle child was two, but already she could calculate odds like lightning, and she picked track winners in her dreams. She ran sucker ads in the papers and had set up a remunerative mail-order business. The youngest was only one and could not yet talk. But he carried chalk and a slate and marked up odds and made book, and was really quite success-ful in a small way. He knew the Four Diamond trick and the Two Story Chicken Coop, the Thimbling Reverse and the Canal Boat Cut. They were intelligent children and theirs was a happy home.

* * * *

One day Mazuma said, "We ought to get out of it, Kate."

"Out of what?"

"Get out of the business. Raise the children in a more wholesome atmo-sphere. Buy a farm and settle down."

"You mean the Blue Valley Farmer trick? Is it old enough to be new yet? And it takes nearly three weeks to set it up, and it never did pay too well for all the trouble."

"No, I do not mean the Blue Valley Farmer trick. I don't mean any trick, swindle, or con. I think we should get out of the whole grind and go to work like honest people."

And when she heard these terrible words Katie fell into a dead faint.

* * * *

That is all of it. He was not a Wreck. He was a common trickster and he had caught the sickness of repentance. The bottom had fallen out of the world indeed. The three unsolvable problems of the Greeks were squaring the circle, trisecting the angle, and re-bottoming the world. They cannot be done.

* * * *

They have been separated for many years. The three children were reared by their father under the recension and curse of Adam. One is a professor of mathematics, but I doubt if he can figure odds as rapidly as he could when he was one year old. The middle one is now a grand lady, but she has lost the facility of picking track winners in her dreams and much else that made her charming. And the oldest one is a senator from a state that I despise.

And Katie is now the wisest old witch in Wreckville. But she has never quite been forgiven her youthful indiscretion when she married an Adamite who felt like his ancient father and deigned to work for a living.

THE UGLY SEA

"The sea is ugly," said Sour John, "and it's peculiar that I'm the only one who ever noticed it. There have been millions of words written on the sea, but nobody has written this. For a time I thought it was just my imagination, that it was only ugly to me. Then I analyzed it and found that it really is ugly.

"It is foul. It is dirtier than a cesspool; yet men who would not willingly bathe in a cesspool will bathe in it. It has the aroma of an open sewer; yet those who would not make a pilgrimage to a sewer will do so to the sea. It is untidy; it is possibly the most untidy thing in the world. And I doubt if there is any practical way to improve it. It cannot be drained; it cannot be covered up; it can only be ignored.

"Everything about it is ignoble. Its animals are baser than those of the land. Its plant life is rootless and protean. It contaminates and wastes the shores. It is an open grave where the living lie down with dead."

"It does smell a little, Sour John, and it is untidy. But I don't think it's ugly. You cannot deny that sometimes it is really beautiful."

"I do deny it. It has no visual beauty. It is monotonous, with only four or five faces, and all of them coarse. The sun and the sky over it may be beautiful; the land that it borders may be fair; but the old sewer itself is ugly."

"Then why are you the only one who thinks so?"

"There could be several reasons. One, that I've long suspected, is that I'm smarter than other people. And another is that mankind has just decided to deny this ugliness for subconscious reasons, which is to say for no reason at all. The sea is a lot like the subconscious. It may even be the subconscious; that was the teaching of the Thalassalogians. The Peoples of the Plains dreamed of the Sea before they visited it. They were guilty dreams. They knew the sea was there, and they were ashamed of it. The Serpent in the Garden was a Hydra, a water snake. He ascended the river to its source to prove that nothing was beyond his reach. That is the secret we have always to live with: that even the rivers of Paradise flow finally into that evil grave. We are in rhythm with the old ocean: it rises irregularly twice in twenty-four hours, and then repents of rising; and so largely do we."

"Sour John, I will still love the sea though you say it is ugly."

"So will I. I did not say I did not love it. I only said it was ugly. It is an open secret that God was less pleased with the sea than with anything else he made. His own people, at least, have always shunned it.

"O, they use it, and several times they have nearly owned it. But they do not go to sea as seamen. In all history there have been only three Jewish seamen. One was in Solomon's navy; he filled a required berth, and was unhappy. One served a Caliph in the tenth century; why I do not know. And the third was Moysha Uferwohner."

"Then let us hear about Moysha."

"Moysha was quite a good man. That is what makes it sad. And the oddest thing is what attracted him to the evil sea. You could not guess it in ten years."

"Not unless it was a waterfront woman."

"That is fantastic. Of all unlikely things that would seem the most un-likely. And yet it's the truth and you hit it at once. Not a woman in being, however, but in potential (as the philosophers have it); which is to say, quite a young girl.

"Likely you have run across her. So I will tell it all."

* * * *

This begins ten years ago. Moysha was then a little short of his major-ity, and was working with his father in an honorable trade not directly con-nected with the sea, that of the loan shark. But they often loaned money to seamen, a perilous business, for which reason the rates were a little higher than you might expect.

Moysha was making collections and picking up a little new trade. This took him to the smell of the sea, which was painful to him, as to any sen-sible man. And it took him to the Blue Fish, a waterfront café, bar, and lodging house.

A twelve-year-old girl, a cripple, the daughter of the proprietor, was playing the piano. It was not for some time, due to the primacy of other matters, that Moysha realized that she was playing atrociously. Then he at-tempted to correct it. "Young lady, one should play well or not at all. Please play better, or stop. That is acutely painful."

She looked as though she were going to cry, and this disconcerted Moysha, though he did not know why it did. Half an hour later the fact intruded itself on his consciousness that she was still playing, and still play-ing badly; but now with a stilted sort of badness.

"Young lady, this is past all bearing. I suggest that you stop playing the damned thing and go to your bed. Or go anywhere and do anything. But this is hideous. Stop it!"

The little girl really did cry then. And as a result of it Moysha got into an altercation, got his head bloodied, and was put out of the place; the first time that such a thing had ever happened to him. Then he realized that the seamen liked the little girl, and liked the way she played the piano.

This does not seem like a good beginning for either a tender love or a great passion. But it had to be the beginning; that was the first time they ever saw each other.

For the next three days Moysha was restless. A serpent was eating at his liver and he could not identify it. He began to take a drink in the middle of the day (it had not been his custom); and on the third day he asked for rum. There was a taste in his mouth and he was trying to match it. And in the inner windings of his head there was an awful smell, and it made him lonesome.

By the evening of the third day the terrible truth came to him: he had to go down for another whiff of that damned sea; and he possibly could not live through another night unless he heard that pretty little girl play the piano again.

Bonny was pretty. She had a wise way with her, and a willful look. It was as though she had just decided not to do something very mean, and was a little sorry that she hadn't.

She didn't really play badly; just out of tune and as nobody else had ever played, with a great amount of ringing in the ballad tunes and a sudden muting, then a sort of clashing and chiming. But she stopped playing when she saw that Moysha was in the room.

Moysha did not get on well at the Blue Fish. He didn't know how to break into the conversation of the seamen, and in his embarrassment he ordered drink after drink. When finally he became quarrelsome (as he had never been before) they put him out of the place again.

Moysha lay on a dirty tarp out on a T head and listened while Bonny played the piano again. Then she stopped. She had probably been sent to bed.

But instead she came out to the T head where he was.

"You old toad, you give me the creeps."

"I do, little girl?"

"Sure you do. And papa says 'Don't let that Yehude in the place again, he makes everybody nervous, if someone wants to borrow money from him let them borrow it somewhere else.' Even the dogs growl at you down here."

"I know it."

"Then why do you come here?"

"Tonight is the only time I ever did come except on business."

"Tonight is what I am talking about."

"I came down to see you."

"I know you did, dear. O, I didn't mean to call you that. I call everybody that."

"Do you want to take it back?"

"No, I don't want to take it back. You old toad, why aren't you a seaman like everybody else?"

"Is everybody else a seaman?"

"Everybody that comes to the Blue Fish. How will you come to the Fish now when Papa won't let you in the place?"

"I don't know."

"If you give me one of your cards I'll call you up."

"Here."

"And if you give me two dollars and a half I'll pay you back three dollars and a quarter Saturday."

"Here."

"I can't play the piano any other way. If you were a seaman I bet you'd like the way I play the piano. Good night, you old toad."

"Good night, Bonny."

And it was then that the dismal thought first came to Moysha: "What if I should be a seaman after all?"

Now this was the most terrible thing he could have done. He could have become a Christian, he could have married a tramp, he could have been convicted of embezzlement. But to leave his old life for the sea would be more than he could stand and more than his family could stand.

And there was no reason for it: only that a twelve-year-old girl looked at him less kindly than if he had been a seaman. It is a terrible and empty thing to go to sea: all order is broken up and there are only periods of debauchery and boredom and work and grinding idleness, and the sickening old pond and its dirty borders. It was for such reasons that Moysha hesitated for three months.

Bonny came to see him for possibly the tenth time. She was now paying him interest of sixty cents a week on an old debt which, in the normal state of affairs, she would never be able to clear.

"Bonny, I wish there was something that I could say to you."

"You can say anything you want to me."

"O Bonny, you don't know what I mean."

"You want to bet I don't?"

"Bonny, what will you be doing in four years?"

"I'll be getting married to a seaman if I can find one to take me."

"Why shouldn't one take you?"

"For a seaman it is bad luck to marry a crippled woman."

So on the first day of summer Moysha went off to sea as a lowly wiper. It broke his heart and shamed his family. He woke and slept in misery for the foulness of the life. He ate goy food and sinned in the ports in attempting to be a salty dog. And it was nine weeks before he was back to his home port; and he went to the Blue Fish with some other seamen.

It was afternoon, and Bonny went for a walk with him across the peninsula and down to the beach.

"Well, I'm thunderstruck is all I can say. Why in the world would a sensible man want to go to sea?"

"I thought you liked seamen, Bonny."

"I do. But how is a man going to turn into a seaman if he isn't one to start with? A dog could turn into a fish easier. That's the dumbest thing anyone ever did. I had an idea when you came to the place today that you turned into a seaman just for me. Did you?"

"Yes."

"I could be coy and say 'Why Moysha, I'm only twelve years old,' but I already knew how you felt. I will tell you something. I never did a mean thing, and I never saw anybody I wanted to be mean to till I met you. But I could be mean to you. It would be fun to ruin you. We aren't good for each other. You oughtn't to see me ever again."

"I have to."

"Then maybe I have to be mean to you. It's for both of us that I ask you not to see me again. I don't want to ruin you, and I don't want to be a mean woman; but I will be if you keep coming around."

"Well, I can't stay away."

"Very well, then I'll be perverse. I'll shock you every time I open my mouth. I'll tell you that I do filthy things, and you won't know whether I'm lying or not. You won't know what I mean, and you'll be afraid to find out. You'll never be able to stay away from me if you don't stay away now. I'll have husbands and still keep you on a string. You'll stand outside in the dark and look at the light in my window, and you'll eat your own heart. Please go away. I don't want to turn mean."

"But Bonny, it doesn't have to be that way."

"I hope it doesn't, but it scares me every time I see you. Now I'll make a bargain with you. If you try to stay away I'll try to stay good. But if you come back again I won't be responsible. You ought to go back uptown and not try to be a seaman any more."

After that the little girl went back to the Blue Fish.

Moysha did not go back uptown. He returned to the sea, and he did not visit that port again for a year. And there was a change in him. From closer acquaintance he no longer noticed that the sea was foul. Once at sunset, for a moment, he found something pleasant about it. He no longer sinned excessively in the ports. Ashore he traveled beyond the waterfront bars and visited the countries behind and met the wonderful people. He got the feel of the rough old globe in his head. In a pension in Holland he played chess with another girl, who was not precocious, and who did not dread turning into a mean woman. In a pub in Denmark he learned to take snuff like the saltiest seaman of them all. In an inn in Brittany he was told that the sea is the heritage of the poor who cannot afford the land. It was in Brittany that he first noticed that he now walked like an old salt.

After a year he went back to his home port and to the Blue Fish.

"In a way I'm glad to see you," said Bonny. "I've been feeling contrary lately and you'll give me an excuse. Every morning I wake up and say 'This day I'm going to raise hell.' Then I can't find anyone to raise hell with. All those water rats I like so well that I can't be mean to them. But I bet I know how to be mean to you. Well go get a room and tell me where it is, and I'll come to you tonight."

"But you're only a little girl, and besides you don't mean it."

"Then you're going to find out if I mean it. I intend to come. If you think you love me because I'm pretty and good, then I'll make you love me for a devil. There's things you don't even know about, and you've been a seaman for a year. I'll make you torture me, and it'll be a lot worse torture to you. I'll show you what unnatural really means. You're going to be mighty sorry you came back."

"Bonny, your humor is cruel."

"When did I ever have any humor? And you don't know if I'm kidding, and you never will know. Would you rather I did these things with someone else than with you?"

"No."

"Well I will. If you don't tell me where your room is, I'll go to someone else's room tonight. I'll do things so filthy you wouldn't believe it. And even if I don't go to somebody, I'll tell you tomorrow that I did."

But Moysha would not tell her where his room was. So late that night when he left the Blue Fish she followed him. It was fantastic for a grown man to walk faster and faster to escape a thirteen-year-old crippled girl, and finally to run in panic through the dark streets. But when finally she lost him she cried out with surprising kindness: "Goodnight Moysha, I'm sorry I was mean."

But she wasn't very sorry, for the next night she was still mean.

"You see that old man with the hair in his ears? He's filthy and we don't even understand each other's language. But he understood what I wanted well enough. He's the one I spent last night with."

"Bonny, that's a lie, and it isn't funny."

"I know it isn't funny. But can you be sure that it's a lie? I only lie part of the time, and you never know when. Now tonight, if you don't tell me where your room is, I'm going to take either that old red-faced slobberer or that black man. And you can follow me, since you run away when I follow you, and see that I go with one of them. And you can stand out in the street and look up at our light. I always leave the light on."

"Bonny, why are you mean?"

"I wish I knew, Moysha, I wish I knew."

* * * *

After a week of this he went to sea again, and did not come back to his home port for two years. He learned of the sea-leaning giants.

"I do not know the name of this tree," said Sour John, "though once I knew it. This is the time of a story where one usually says it's time for a drink. However, for a long time I have been worried about my parasites who are to me almost like my own children, and this constant diet of rum and redeye cannot be good for them. I believe if the young lady would fry me a platter of eggs it would please my small associates, and do me more good than harm."

He learned, Moysha did, of the sea-leaning giants. They are massive trees of the islands and the more fragmentary mainlands, and they grow almost horizontal out toward the sea. They are not influenced by the wind; from the time they are little whips the wind is always blowing in from the sea, and they grow against it and against all reason. They have, some of them, trunks nine feet thick, but they always lean out over the sea. Moysha began to understand why they did, though most people would never understand it.

He acquired a talking bird of great versatility. He acquired also a ring-tailed monkey and a snake that he carried around inside his shirt, for Moysha was now a very salty seaman.

He was prosperous, for he had never forsaken the trade of the money-lender, and he was always a shrewd buyer of novelties and merchandise. He turned them over as he went from port to port, and always at a profit.

He became a cool student of the ceaseless carnage of the ocean, and loved to muse on the ascending and descending corpses and their fragments in the old watery grave.

He spent seven months on a certain Chinese puzzle, and he worked it, the only Occidental who ever had patience enough to do so.

* * * *

When she was fifteen Bonny married a seaman, and he was not Moysha. This happened just one week before Moysha came back to port and to the Blue Fish. The man she married was named Oglesby Ogburn; and if you think that's a funny name, you should have heard the handles of some of them that she turned down.

The very day that Moysha came to the Blue Fish was the day that Oglesby left; for the honeymoon was over, and he had to go back to the sea. Bonny was now all kindness to everyone. But she still put the old needle into Moysha.

"I've had a husband for a week now, so I won't be able to get along without a man. You stay with me while you're in town; and after that I'll get another, and then another and another. And by that time Oglesby will be back for a week."

"Don't talk like that, Bonny, even if I know you're joking."

"But you don't know that I'm joking. You never know for sure."

"How can anyone who looks so like an angel talk like that?"

"It does provide a contrast. Don't you think it makes me more interesting? I didn't know you were the kind who chased married women."

"I'm not. But O Bonny! What am I to do?"

"Well I've certainly offered you everything. I don't know how I can offer you any more."

And a few days later when Moysha was leaving port they talked again.

"You haven't even given me a wedding present or wished me luck. And we do need it. It's always bad luck for a seaman to marry a crippled woman. What are you going to give me for a wedding present?"

"The only thing I will give you is the serpent from my bosom."

"O don't talk so flowery."

Then he took the snake out of his shirt.

"O, I didn't know you had a real snake. Is he for me? That's the nicest present anyone ever gave me. What do you call him?"

"Why, just a snake. Ular, that is, he's a foreign snake."

So he went back to sea and left the little girl there with the snake in her hands.

Bonny was a widow when she was sixteen, as everyone had known she would be. It's no joke about it being bad luck for a seaman to marry a cripple. They seldom lose much time in perishing after they do it. Oglesby died at sea, as all the Ogburns did; and it was from a trifling illness from which he was hardly sick at all. It was many weeks later that Moysha heard the news, and then he hurried back to his home port.

He was too late. Bonny had married again.

"I thought you'd probably come, and I kind of wanted it to be you. But you waited so long, and the summer was half over, that I decided to marry Polycarp Melish. I'm halfway sorry I did. He wouldn't let Ular sleep with us, and he killed him just because he bit him on the thumb.

"But I tell you what you do. What with the bad luck and all, Polycarp won't last many months. Come around earlier next year. I like to get married in the springtime. I'll be a double widow then."

"Bonny, that's a terrible way to talk even when kidding."

"I'm not kidding at all. I even have an idea how we can beat the jinx. I'll tell you about it after we get married next year. Maybe a crippled girl gets to keep her third husband."

"Do you want Polycarp to die?"

"Of course I don't. I love him. I love all my husbands, just like I'll love you after I marry you. I can't help it if I'm bad luck. I told him, and he said he already knew it; but he wanted to do it anyhow. Will you bring me another snake the next time you're in port?"

"Yes. And you can keep the monkey in place of it till I come back. But you can't have the bird yet. I have to keep someone to talk to."

"All right. Please come in the spring. Don't wait till summer again or it'll be too late and I'll already be married to someone else. But whether we get married or not, I'm never going to be mean again. I'm getting too old for that."

So he went to sea again happier than he ever had before.

When she was seventeen Bonny was a widow again as everyone had known she would be. Polycarp had been mangled and chopped to pieces in an unusual accident in the engine room of his ship.

Moysha heard of it very soon, before it could have been heard of at home. And he took council with his talking bird, and with one other, technically more human.

"This other," said Sour John, "was myself. It was very early spring, and Moysha was wondering if it were really best to hurry home and marry Bonny.

"'I am not at all superstitious,' he said. 'I do not believe that a crippled woman is necessarily bad luck to seamen. But I believe that Bonny may be bad luck to everyone, including herself.'

"We were on a chocolate island of a French flavor and a French name. On it were girls as pretty as Bonny, and without her reputation for bad luck: girls who would never be either wives or widows. And there is a way to go clear around the world from one such place to another.

"'The Blue Fish is not necessarily the center of the earth,' I told him. 'I have always necessarily believed them to be a little left of center. And Bonny may not be the queen. But if you think that she is, then for you she is so. Nine months, or even a year is not very long to live, and you will be at sea most of the time. But if you think a few weeks with the little girl is enough, then it is enough for you. A lot of others who will not have even that will be dead by next Easter.' I said this to cheer him up. I was always the cheerful type.

"'And what do you think?' Moysha asked the talking bird.

"'Sampah,' said the bird in his own tongue. This means rubbish. But whether he meant that the superstition was rubbish, or the idea of marrying with a consequent early death was rubbish, is something that is still locked up in his little green head."

Moysha hurried home to marry Bonny. He brought a brother of Ular for a present, and he went at once to the Blue Fish.

"Well you're just in time. I was going to have the banns read for me and somebody tomorrow, and if you'd been an hour later it wouldn't have been you.

"I was halfway afraid to come."

"You needn't have been afraid. I told you I knew a way to beat the jinx. I'm selling the Blue Fish. I wrote you that Papa was dead. And we're going to take a house uptown and forget the sea."

"Forget the sea? How could anyone forget the sea?"

"Why, you're only a toy seaman. You weren't raised to it. When you go away from it you won't be a seaman at all. And crippled women are only bad luck to seamen, not to other men."

"But what would I do? The sea is all I know."

"Don't be a child, Moysha. You hate the sea, remember? You always told me that you did. You only went to sea because you thought I liked seamen. You know a hundred ways to make a dollar, and you don't have to go near the sea for any of them."

So they were married. And they were happy. Moysha discovered that Bonny was really an angel. Her devil talk had been a stunt.

It was worth all five dark years at sea to have her. She was now even more lovely than the first night he had seen her. They lived in a house uptown in the heart of the city, and were an urbane and civilized couple. And three years went by.

Then one day Bonny said that they ought to get rid of the snake, and maybe even the monkey. She was afraid they would bite one of the children, or one of the children would bite them.

The talking bird said that if his friends left he would leave, too.

"But Bonny," said Moysha, "these three are all that I have to remind me of the years when I was a seaman.

"You have me, also. But why do you want to be reminded of those awful days?"

"I know what we could do, Bonny. We could buy the Blue Fish again. It isn't doing well. We could live there and run it. And we could have a place there for the snake and the monkey and the bird."

"Yes, we could have a place for them all, but not for the children. That is no place to raise children. I know, and I was raised there. Now my love, don't be difficult. Take the three creatures and dispose of them. And remember that for us the sea isn't even there any more."

But it was still there when he went down to the Blue Fish to try to sell the three creatures to the seaman. An old friend of his was present and was looking for an engineer first class to ship out that very night. And there was a great difficulty in selling the creatures.

He could not sell them unless he put a price on them, and he was damned if he'd do that. That was worse than putting a price on his own children. He had had them longer than his children, and they were more peculiarly his own. He could not sell them. And he could not go home and tell his wife that he could not sell them.

* * * *

"He went out and sat on the horns of the dilemma and looked at the sea. And then his old friend (who coincidentally was myself)," said Sour John, "came out and said that he sure did need an engineer first class to leave that very night.

"And then what do you think that Moysha did?"

"O, he signed on and went back to sea."

Sour John was thunderstruck.

"How did you know that? You've hit it again. I never will know how you do it. Well, that's what he did. In the face of everything he left his beautiful wife and children, and his clean life, and went to the filthy sea again. It's incredible."

"And how is he doing now?"

"God knows. I mean it literally. Naturally he's dead. That's been a year. You don't expect a seaman married to a crippled woman to live forever do you?"

"And how is Bonny?"

"I went to see her this afternoon; for this is the port where it all happened. She had out an atlas and a pencil and piece of string. She was trying to measure out what town in the whole country is furthest from the sea.

"She is lonely and grieves for Moysha, more than for either of her other husbands. But O she is lovely! She supports herself and her brood by giving piano lessons."

"Is there a moral to this?"

"No. It is an immoral story. And it's a mystery to me. A man will not normally leave a clean home to dwell in an open grave, nor abandon children to descend into a sewer, nor forswear a lovely and loving wife to go faring on a cesspool, knowing that he will shortly die there as a part of the bargain.

"But that is what he did."

SEVEN-DAY TERROR

"Is there anything you want to make disappear?" Clarence Willoughby asked his mother.

"A sink full of dishes is all I can think of. How will you do it?"

"I just built a disappearer. All you do is cut the other end out of a beer can. Then you take two pieces of red cardboard with peepholes in the middle and fit them in the ends. You look through the peepholes and blink. Whatever you look at will disappear."

"Oh."

"But I don't know if I can make them come back. We'd better try it on something else. Dishes cost money."

As always, Myra Willoughby had to admire the wisdom of her nine-year-old son. She would not have had such foresight herself. He always did. "You can try it on Blanche Manners' cat outside there. Nobody will care if it disappears except Blanche Manners."

"All right."

He put the disappearer to his eye and blinked. The cat disappeared from the sidewalk outside.

His mother was interested. "I wonder how it works. Do you know how it works?"

"Yes. You take a beer can with both ends cut out and put in two pieces of cardboard. Then you blink."

"Never mind. Take it outside and play with it. You hadn't better make anything disappear in here till I think about this."

But when he had gone his mother was oddly disturbed.

"I wonder if I have a precocious child. Why, there's lots of grown people who wouldn't know how to make a disappearer that would work. I wonder if Blanche Manners will miss her cat very much?"

Clarence went down to the Plugged Nickel, a pot house on the corner.

"Do you have anything you want to make disappear, Nokomis?"

"Only my paunch."

"If I make it disappear it'll leave a hole in you and you'll bleed to death."

"That's right, I would. Why don't you try it on the fireplug outside?"

This in a way was one of the happiest afternoons ever in the neighborhood. The children came from blocks around to play in the flooded streets and gutters, and if some of them drowned (and we don't say that they did drown) in the flood (and brother! it was a flood), why you have to expect things like that. The fire engines (whoever heard of calling fire engines to put out a flood?) were apparatus-deep in water. The policemen and ambulance men wandered around wet and bewildered.

"Resuscitator, resuscitator, anybody wanna resuscitator," chanted Clarissa Willoughby.

"Oh, shut up," said the ambulance attendants.

Nokomis, the bar man in the Plugged Nickel, called Clarence inside.

"I don't believe, just for the moment, I'd tell anyone what happened to that fireplug."

"I won't tell if you won't tell," said Clarence.

Officer Comstock was suspicious. "There's only seven possible explanations: one of the seven Willoughby kids did it. I dunno how. It'd take a bulldozer to do it, and then there'd be something left of the plug. But however they did it, one of them did it."

Officer Comstock had a talent for getting near the truth of dark matters. This is why he was walking a beat out here in the boondocks instead of sitting in a chair downtown.

"Clarissa!" said Officer Comstock in a voice like thunder.

"Resuscitator, resuscitator, anybody wanna resuscitator?" chanted Clarissa.

"Do you know what happened to that fireplug?" asked Officer C.

"I have an uncanny suspicion. As yet it is no more than that. When I am better informed I will advise you."

Clarissa was eight years old and much given to uncanny suspicions.

"Clementine, Harold, Corinne, Jimmy, Cyril," he asked the five younger Willoughby children. "Do you know what happened to that fireplug?"

"There was a man around yesterday. I bet he took it," said Clementine.

"I don't even remember a fireplug there. I think you're making a fuss about nothing," said Harold.

"City hall's going to hear about this," said Corinne.

"Pretty dommed sure," said Jimmy, "but I won't tell."

"Cyril!" cried Officer Comstock in a terrible voice. Not a terrifying voice, a terrible voice. He felt terrible now.

"Great green bananas," said Cyril, "I'm only three years old. I don't see how it's even my responsibility."

"Clarence," said Officer Comstock.

Clarence gulped.

"Do you know where the fireplug went?"

Clarence brightened. "No, sir. I don't know where it went."

A bunch of smart alecs from the water department came out and shut off the water for a few blocks around and put some kind of cap on in place of the fireplug. "This sure is going to be a funny-sounding report," said one of them.

Officer Comstock walked away discouraged. "Don't bother me, Miss Manners," he said. "I don't know where to look for your cat. I don't even know where to look for a fireplug."

"I have an idea," said Clarissa, "that when you find the cat you will find the fireplug in the same place. As yet it's only an idea."

Ozzie Murphy wore a little hat on top of his head. Clarence pointed his weapon and winked. The hat was no longer there, but a little trickle of blood was running down the pate.

"I don't believe I'd play with that any more," said Nokomis.

"Who's playing?" said Clarence. "This is for real."

This was the beginning of the seven-day terror in the heretofore obscure neighborhood. Trees disappeared from the parks; lamp posts were as though they had never been; Wally Waldorf drove home, got out, slammed the door of his car, and there was no car. As George Mullendorf came up the walk to his house his dog Pete ran to meet him and took a flying leap to his arms. The dog left the sidewalk but something happened; the dog was gone and only a bark lingered for a moment in the puzzled air.

But the worst were the fireplugs. The second plug was installed the morning after the disappearance of the first. In eight minutes it was gone and the flood waters returned. Another one was in by twelve o'clock. Within three minutes it had vanished. The next morning fireplug number four was installed.

The water commissioner was there, the city engineer was there, the chief of police was there with a riot squad, the president of the Parent-Teachers Association was there, the president of the university was there, the mayor was there, three gentlemen of the FBI, a newsreel photographer, eminent scientists and a crowd of honest citizens.

"Let's see it disappear now," said the city engineer.

"Let's see it disappear now," said the police chief.

"Let's see it disa—it did, didn't it?" said one of the eminent scientists.

And it was gone and everybody was very wet.

"At least I have the picture sequence of the year," said the photographer. But his camera and apparatus disappeared from the midst of them.

"Shut off the water and cap it," said the commissioner. "And don't put in another plug yet. That was the last plug in the warehouse."

"This is too big for me," said the mayor. "I wonder that Tass doesn't have it yet."

"Tass has it," said a little round man. "I am Tass."

"If all of you gentlemen will come into the Plugged Nickel," said Nokomis, "and try one of our new Fire Hydrant Highballs you will all be happier. These are made of good corn whiskey, brown sugar, and hydrant water from this very gutter. You can be the first to drink them."

Business was phenomenal at the Plugged Nickel, for it was in front of its very doors that the fireplugs disappeared in floods of gushing water.

"I know a way we can get rich," said Clarissa several days later to her father, Tom Willoughby. "Everybody says there going to sell their houses for nothing and move out of the neighborhood. Go get a lot of money and buy them all. Then you can sell them again and get rich."

"I wouldn't buy them for a dollar each. Three of them have disappeared already, and all the families but us have their furniture moved out in their front yards. There might be nothing but vacant lots in the morning."

"Good, then buy the vacant lots. And you can be ready when the houses come back."

"Come back? Are the houses going to come back? Do you know anything about this, young lady?"

"I have a suspicion verging on a certainty. As of now I can say no more."

* * * *

Three eminent scientists were gathered in an untidy suite that looked as though it belonged to a drunken sultan.

"This transcends the metaphysical. It impinges on the quantum continuum. In some way it obsoletes Boff," said Dr. Velikof Vonk.

"The contingence of the intransigence is the most mystifying aspect," said Arpad Arkbaranan.

"Yes," said Willy McGilly. "Who would have thought that you could do it with a beer can and two pieces of cardboard? When I was a boy I used an oatmeal box and red crayola."

"I do not always follow you," said Dr. Vonk. "I wish you would speak plainer."

So far no human had been injured or disappeared—except for a little blood on the pate of Ozzie Murphy, on the lobes of Conchita when her gaudy earrings disappeared from her very ears, a clipped flinger or so when a house vanished as the front doorknob was touched, a lost toe when a neighborhood boy kicked a can and the can was not; probably not more than a pint of blood and three or four ounces of flesh all together.

Now, however, Mr. Buckle the grocery man disappeared before witnesses. This was serious.

Some mean-looking investigators from downtown came out to the Willoughbys. The meanest-looking one was the mayor. In happier days he had not been a mean man, but the terror had now reigned for seven days.

"There have been ugly rumors," said one of the mean investigators, "that link certain events to this household. Do any of you know anything about them?"

"I started most of them," said Clarissa. "But I didn't consider them ugly. Cryptic, rather. But if you want to get to the bottom of this just ask me a question."

"Did you make those things disappear?" asked the investigator.

"That isn't the question," said Clarissa.

"Do you know where they have gone?" asked the investigator.

"That isn't the question either," said Clarissa.

"Can you make them come back?"

"Why, of course I can. Anybody can. Can't you?"

"I cannot. If you can, please do so at once."

"I need some stuff. Get me a gold watch and a hammer. Then go down to the drug store and get me this list of chemicals. And I need a yard of black velvet and a pound of rock candy."

"Shall we?" asked one of the investigators.

"Yes," said the mayor. "It's our only hope. Get her anything she wants."

And it was all assembled.

"Why does she get all the attention?" asked Clarence. "I was the one who made all the things disappear. How does she know how to get them back?"

"I knew it!" cried Clarissa with hate. "I knew he was the one that did it. He read in my diary how to make a disappearer. If I was his mother I'd whip him for reading his little sister's diary. That's what happens when things like that fall into irresponsible hands."

She poised the hammer over the mayor's gold watch, now on the floor.

"I have to wait a few seconds. This can't be hurried. It'll only be a little while."

The second hand swept around to the point that was preordained for it before the world began. Clarissa suddenly brought down the hammer with all her force on the beautiful gold watch.

"That's all," she said. "Your troubles are over. See, there is Blanche Manners' cat on the sidewalk just where she was seven days ago."

And the cat was back.

"Now let's go down to the Plugged Nickel and watch the fireplugs come back."

They had only a few minutes to wait. It came from nowhere and clanged into the street like a sign and a witness.

"Now I predict," said Clarissa, "that every single object will return exactly seven days from the time of its disappearance."

The seven-day terror had ended. The objects began to reappear.

"How," asked the mayor, "did you know they would come back in seven days?"

"Because it was a seven-day disappearer that Clarence made. I also know how to make a nine-day, a thirteen-day, a twenty-seven day, and an eleven-year disappearer. I was going to make a thirteen-year one, but for that you have to color the ends with the blood from a little boy's heart, and Cyril cried every time I tried to make a good cut."

"You really know how to make all of these?"

"Yes. But I shudder if the knowledge should ever come into unauthorized hands."

"I shudder, too, Clarissa. But tell me, why did you want the chemicals?

"For my chemistry set."

"And the black velvet?"

"For doll dresses."

"And the pound of rock candy?"

"How did you ever get to be mayor of this town if you have to ask questions like that? What do you think I wanted the rock candy for?"

"One last question," said the mayor. "Why did you smash my gold watch with the hammer?"

"Oh," said Clarissa, "that was for dramatic effect."

OTHER SIDE OF THE MOON

Johnny O'Conner got off at the same corner every night. Everyone got off at the same corner every night. The old joker with the face like an egg, the noble-nosed Nabob, the stylish old girl who looked like a lady lawyer, all got off at Rambush Street. The wacky Dude who looked like a barber, the nice, plain, blonde girl, the little man who reminded you of an onion, all got off at Scottsboro. And Pauline Potter, fat George Gregoff, the antiseptic Gentleman with a contempt of the world, and Johnny O'Conner himself, always got off at Terhune. This was invariable. Other people got off at other places, but always at the same places.

When Johnny got off, he always ducked into the Loco Club, had a Vodka Collins, then walked the half-block home. Sheila was waiting, and supper was ready in about twelve minutes.

But one night a week ago it had been different. The bus stopped at Scottsboro. The wacky Dude who looked like a barber, the little man who reminded you of an onion, both got off. But the nice, plain, blonde girl just sat there.

"Scottsboro, Miss," said the driver.

"Thank you," said the plain blonde girl, but she just sat there.

"You always get off at Scottsboro, Miss," said the driver.

"Not tonight," said the girl.

So the bus went on, but everybody was uneasy from the incident. The normal order of the world had fallen apart.

Then tonight it happened again. At Scottsboro the wacky Dude and the man who reminded you of an onion got off. And the plain blonde girl said, "not tonight." This was not so startling as the first time it happened, but it did set Johnny O'Conner wondering. It was not as though the old joker with the face like an egg, the noble-nosed nabob, or the stylish old girl who looked like a lady-lawyer had not got off at Rambush. It was not as though Pauline Potter, fat George Gregoff, and the antiseptic gentleman with the contempt of the world were not even now getting off at Terhune.

"Terhune," said the driver. "You always get off at Terhune, Mr. O'Conner."

"Not tonight," said Johnny. This statement startled him. He had not known he was going to say that. He had not known he would ride beyond his own corner. But the bus went on and Johnny did not even know where it was going. He had lived in a house for a year and had never even been to the next street.

"Urbana," said the driver. And here there descended from the bus some of those creatures who before had seemed to have no habitation or true place in the world. The moon-faced man who always carried the Sporting News, the heavy smiling lady who was a picture of placidity, the pale vacuous youth who combined duck-tail and sideburns on one head, the shop-girl with the red hat and the shop-girl with the green hat got off here. And also the nice, plain, blonde girl, who when the world was normal, used to descend at Scottsboro. And Johnny O'Conner to his own amazement got off here, too.

Urbana was not too different from Terhune, although of course in a different world. Instead of the Loco Club there was the Krazy Kat Club Number Two. Johnny went in with only an instant's wonder as to the location of Krazy Kat Number One. He had a Cuba Libra. Then he walked the half-block back to his house. He had never seen his house from this side before. It was like seeing the other side of the moon. And on that other side of the moon the paint had started to crack above one window, and the screen had begun to tear.

"Where have you been?" asked Sheila. "I was frantic."

"How could you be frantic? I am home at the same time as always. Or within forty-five seconds of it."

"But you didn't get off at Terhune Street."

"How do you know I didn't?"

"Pauline Potter told me, and so did George Gregoff, and Mr. Sebastian."

"Who's he?"

She made motions with her hands, and he knew that Mr. Sebastian was the antiseptic gentleman with a contempt of the world. But Sheila was not finished.

"Where did you go? They all said you stayed right on the bus and rode right past your house. Why did you do it? You never did that before."

"Honey, I just rode one block down and then walked back the half-block from the other way."

"But why did you do it? What did you do down there?"

"I went into the Krazy Kat Club Number Two and had one drink, all that I ever had."

"You went into a strange bar? Don't you know that men can get into trouble in a strange bar? What did you drink?"

"I had a Cuba Libra."

"Why did you do that? Only gamblers and seamen ever drink them. You aren't going to run away to sea, are you?"

"I hadn't given it a thought. But it might not be a bad idea."

"Why do you say that? Are you really going to leave me?"

"Sheila, honey, that was only a joke."

"Why do you do that? You never made a joke before. I just don't know what to make of you."

And even then it wasn't over. At supper she kept it up.

"Promise me, Johnny, that you won't ever do a thing like that again."

"But I didn't do anything. Only rode one block past my stop and walked half-a-block back home."

"And went into a strange bar where there's no telling what might happen to you. Promise me you will never go there again. I have a reason. Promise me."

"I solemnly promise," said Johnny O'Conner, "that I will never again go to the Krazy Kat Club Number Two. But if I ever come to that Number One Kat look out."

"There you go, making a joke again. I just don't know what has come over you."

The next night Johnny was in a wayward mood. It wasn't just that he had an unreasonable wife. Generally, he enjoyed his unreasonable wife. But a little bee was buzzing in his bonnet. He had had a glimpse over the top of his rut and he wondered what was in the world beyond. He had an almost overpowering compulsion to get off at Manderville where the untidy old duffer and the two young girls always got off. He barely mastered himself at Nassau, and as he passed Oswego it was with the gravest uneasiness. Then he decided in his mind, and he watched the plain blonde girl. If she goes past her stop I will go past mine, he thought. At Patrick, the bald-headed coot with hair in his ears and the frazzled cigar in the front of his face got out, and that was as it should be. At Quarles their party was diminished by Laughing Boy, by Dapper Dan, by the Sniffler, and by a person who may or may not have been Tug-Boat Annie.

At Rambush it was egg-face, nabob, and lady-lawyer, and the world was rolling tolerably in its groove. But the end was not yet. For at Scottsboro the wacky Dude and the little man who was cousin of the onion got off, and the plain blonde girl did not. This is it, thought Johnny O'Conner. I'll go past mine, too. I may go two blocks past and see what Vandalia is like. I may go all the way to the end of the world or the end of the alphabet, whichever one comes first. For Johnny was in a reckless mood.

At Terhune he endured the insulting sniff of Pauline Potter, the glowering of fat George Gregoff, the withering contempt of the antiseptic gentleman, now know as Mr. Sebastian. Johnny stared ahead and remained on the bus. The nice, plain, blonde girl got off again at Urbana, and Johnny got off there, too. The blonde girl went into the Krazy Kat club Number Two and Johnny broke his promise to his wife and went in also. He ordered a Sazarac to see what it was like and gazed with new eyes at a new world.

"I'm glad you came this evening," the bar-maid told the nice, plain, blonde girl. "You're the only one of my old friends who ever get this far out. This is a mean afternoon. I'm glad to see someone nice."

"Is it mean out here? I thought after the places you worked this would be a breeze."

"Girl, I have one screw-ball worse than anything I ever had downtown. That woman makes me ashamed. She has three different dates here every afternoon. The first one is with that fat, old bumbler. The way they carry on in a booth I told them today I'd have to call the cops if they didn't tone it down. They both always get sloppy drunk, and when he leaves he always gives her money. As soon as he's gone, there's another one comes in that looks like a tough boy out of an old George Raft movie. This time she gives the money to him and they put on a little show that sure wouldn't get past the censors. It's real purple stuff those two put on. And when he's pretty drunk he goes. And in about twenty minutes her third date comes in. They each drink three fast ones. Then they get in his car and are gone for an hour. When they come back, they each have three more fast ones. He leaves then and she staggers back to one of the booths and goes to sleep."

"How does she get away with it?"

"She says she has her husband trained. Has him so deep in a rut he can't see over the top and never will catch on. But she's smart. She's never so drunk that the little clock inside her head doesn't work. She hears that five-thirty bus when it squeaks to a stop down at Terhune. Then she jumps up, calls me a couple of dirty names just to keep in practice, and goes out the back door and down the alley to her house. She's always there when her husband gets home. We had some tramps downtown but we never had any as bad as Sheila O'Conner."

Johnny O'Conner shook and spilled his chaser. He had left his rut and now he could not go back to it. All he could do was go to the end of the alphabet or the end of the world. He had seen his home from the other side. He had seen the other side of the moon. And he was appalled.

DAY OF THE GLACIER

The Fifth or Zurichthal glaciation of the Pleistocene began on the morning of April 1, 1962, on a Sunday about nine o'clock by eastern time. This was about twenty-five hours earlier than Doctor Ergodic Eimer had calculated; it threw him into panic, as his preparations were not entirely completed.

Lesser persons had been thrown into a panic nearly an hour before by a series of lesser events. And yet on an ordinary day they would have been of major magnitude.

It was that the thirty-three ICBM launching buses of the United States and Canada had been destroyed simultaneously. Full details were not immediately available, and now due to subsequent catastrophes they are lost forever.

Radio and TV news flashes tried to give a warning and fragmentary details, but on every channel and frequency the same cool voice would always cut in: "This is an April Fools Day simulated news broadcast. Do not be alarmed. This program is fictional."

Congress had been in session for three months, and the new Peace Faction was completely dominant. As is known to all who are acquainted with Mergendal's Law of Parliamentary Subversion, in all of the once free countries that had succumbed to the Controlled Statists (now thirty-seven) it was subsequently discovered that twenty percent of the elected had clandestinely been working for the Controlled Statists all along; that sixty percent had no true principles or basis of belief of any sort and no practical aim except to be on the winning side, and that a final twenty percent were to some degree die-hards, more or less devoted to the old way.

* * * *

Incidentally, at this moment the latter percent had virtually ceased to exist. A series of nearly one hundred mysterious early morning murders in Washington, Chevy Chase, Silver Spring, New York and other not-too-widely scattered locations had done for most of them. This was not widely known even now, several hours later; although curiously the accounts of several of their deaths were in the Metropolitan papers before they happened. In the case of one, at least, it did not happen at all; he had forewarning and was miles away at the time of the attempt.

It had been unseasonably warm and dry for six weeks, for which reason nearly everyone except Doctor Ergodic Eimer and his cronies were surprised by the sudden chill and quick heavy snow.

They were in feverish preparation, having to telescope many hours of work into one. When they got to the airport, three inches of snow had already fallen, and it was as though it had only begun. They left quickly in three chartered planes, the last ever to leave there.

In the great cities of the Eastern Seaboard, only a little over five inches of snow fell in the first hour; but in the second hour more than seventeen. Many people of the nation seeing the fantastic accumulation simply went to bed for the day. And millions of them stayed there till they died; there was no way out.

America died that week except for a few lingering communities on the Gulf of California, and the lower Mexican deserts, and the snow dusted Indies. Europe died, and most of Asia, and the southern continents froze from the bottom up. Melbourne and Sydney and Port Elizabeth were buried, as well as Buenos Aires; and even Rio right on the tropic had seven feet of snow.

* * * *

"The last time it happened," said Doctor Eimer, "the Padiwire Valley was a good place. We know this from our previous studies and our preparatory expedition there last year."

"Who would have thought," asked Professor Schubert, "that an ice age could have come so suddenly?"

"Apparently only myself," replied the good doctor. "I told everybody worth telling but had very little response for my trouble. It isn't as though we haven't had four very recent ones to study. It isn't as though it weren't written plainly in the rocks for everyone to see. Though I must say," he continued as he shivered in his great coat, "that this was a mighty short inter-glacial—actually less than twenty thousand years of what we might call really nice weather."

"Will it snow long?" asked Violet, his somewhat overcharming secretary. Dr. Eimer often said that he kept Violet for her looks only, as she was not much smarter than the average PhD.

"I think not," he answered. "Possibly not more than ninety thousand years of maintained snow, and the accumulation itself will come in the first fraction of that period; a very short duration. This will be a sort of sport among the ice ages. There is no good reason for it to happen, and it could have been prevented. However, once the balance is tipped, it takes it a little while to swing back. We can be thankful that it will not be as long nor as cold as Wurm."

"Or Mindel or Riss," said Professor Schubert.

"Or Gunz," said Professor Gilluly. "I'd hate to have to go through that one again."

"None of you act as though it were serious," said Violet.

"Yes," said Doctor Eimer, "the world is dying and that is serious. But we will save ourselves, and part of the luggage we take with us is a little good humor. If we are too serious, we will die also. The serious always die first."

* * * *

"What was wrong with your calculations?" asked Professor Schubert. "If we hadn't cut and run for it, we'd never have made it. Another half hour and we'd have been trapped for good."

"My calculations, as always, were perfect. But the balance was so delicate that a bit of unlooked for turbulence set it off."

"Turbulence?"

"Possibly less than two hundred fission warheads that struck our launching bases. Who would have believed that such a little thing could upset the balance a day early. But the balance was delicate."

"LaPlace-Mendira said that an ice age must be preceded by a thirty thousand year cooling-off period."

"LaPlace-Mendira is an idiot. The Siberian mammoths were frozen solid with green grass between their teeth. There was no more a cooling-off period then than now. In ninety or a hundred thousand years from now, black Angus cattle will be found in the Kansas snow frozen solid with green grass in their several stomachs. It will be a wonder—black, proto-bovine animals with incredibly short legs, and looking almost like a cross between a pig and a cow. You know, of course, that all cattle at the beginning of the fifth interglacial will be red, or red and white, and quite tall."

"I had not known that."

"It seems that almost anybody would be able to predict the way the combination color and shoulder-height-coefficient gene would respond under moderately prolonged glacial stress."

"To tell you the truth, Doctor, I've never given it a thought." Professor Gilluly, in some ways, seemed not to have a complete scientific devotion.

"But it never before glaciated the whole surface of the earth."

"Nor will it now."

"But you said that even the Padiwire Valley where we are going will have ice and snow."

"Oh, that is only temporary—a period of so short duration that we can disregard it, except of course to take precautions that we don't freeze to death. I venture that it will not have fallen to within fifteen degrees above zero when we land there, and there will be less than nine inches of snow. You must remember that it is nearly on the equator, and we are less than two weeks from the vernal equinox. The quick-freeze period will last less than ten days. Then the clouds will clear, for the simple reason that all the moisture will have fallen, and the sun will have come through. And here, at least, the snow will somewhat melt—though further north and south it will not.

"For a period of about seven years there will be very heavy snowfall and the ocean depth will drop about five feet a year. Then we enter the next phase—which will last no more than eighty-five years—when the snow will continue to accumulate on earth, but at a reduced rate, and the sea level will drop only about a foot a year. After that, the ice age will be barely able to maintain itself and will essentially be over.

"It is true that the snow will linger for another eighty-thousand years, but it will not greatly increase. And one day it will begin to diminish, and this will be much more rapid than experts believe. Then the oceans will rise at the rate of a foot a year for a hundred years, and a large part of the land will have different and larger rivers, and some former islands will be joined to the mainland, and new islands will be sliced off."

"You can predict ninety-thousand years, but can you tell us what is happening right now? How did the other two planes get ahead of us?"

"If they did, then I can only say that they passed us in the snow for it does look as though two planes have already landed."

"Well, does it look as if we have already landed too?" asked Violet. "There is a third plane down there. Is that us?"

"Obviously it is not. Are you getting light-headed? There are, if you will look closely, at least seven planes there. Well, we have made no preparations for landing elsewhere. We will land as we planned."

And as soon as they touched down they were taken into custody.

* * * *

Nauchnii-Komandir Andreyev, known in scientific circles as the Anagallic, was pleased and perfunctory.

"Ah, liddle Doctor Eimer, is it true you are not a complete idiot? I had thought you were nearly complete. An idiot may, or may not know enough to come in out of the rain, but you have come in out of the snow. You surprise me. As you see we are in total control. These three are your only planes?"

"No. No. We have quite an armada on the way."

"Those who are not practiced should lie little or not at all. But there has been stupidity all around. This morning our leaders thought they would have the whole world in their hand, and this afternoon it is some of their delegates who do have all that will be left of it. It pleases me the way it happened. I would not have changed it if I could. I am now the commander of the world."

"You are not our commander."

"You are dogs. Learn that. We have studied the Eskimo, and one rule they have: the dogs do not sleep in the house or the tent. The dogs grow lazy if they sleep inside. We have your equipment. You are the dogs and you will sleep in the snow and learn your place."

"We will see."

"We have already seen. We have you outnumbered now by three hundred to fifty. It will not always be so we hope—the working dogs should outnumber the men. But our positions will not change. You know (though few others hold theories that coincide with my own) that during the last ice age, the Wurm, there were two types of men or near-men: the Neanderthal who were the masters, and the Grimaldi who were their slaves. We are the new Neanderthalan and you are the new Grimaldi. We had thought to use a few jungle Indian remnants for that, but now we will use you.

"But you must be more numerous. There seems to be only twenty-seven women among you, and my census clerk has just reported that fifteen of them are without mates. This will be corrected. Arrange it among yourselves, but arrange it by nightfall. And remember, we expect fruition within nine months. I believe that in one of your obsoleted books there is a phrase about cutting down the tree that will not bear fruit. And do not any of you get peculiar ideas about resisting. We have with us a sadist group. I shudder at these things myself, but those to whom I delegate them will not shudder."

* * * *

They were in a white and brown world. The savanna vegetation on the fringe of the jungle, unacquainted with frost for thousands of years, withered at its touch. Every growing thing seemed suddenly to die. Yet the snow could not yet cover it all, it was too lush and high and thick; the small trees would bend with its weight, and then spring free and shake it off their crowns, so that when it finally covered them it covered them from the bottom up.

"Can we even live here?" asked Violet. "It seems that we could starve or freeze here as easily as at home. We might not freeze quite as hard, if that is any comfort."

"No, we will do neither," said Gully Gilluly. "We will not have it bad. By dark tonight a million birds will descend on this valley. They will perch on every tree and bush and on the ground. We can knock ten thousand of them in the heads and stack them in the snow.

"We cannot lack for fuel. Enough trees for a hundred years have been struck dead here within several hours. And within ten days there will be better adapted new vegetation start through the old. Dr. Eimer says this always happens; that seeds that have been here dormant since Wurm will now come to life. And by that time there will be patches through the snow. We will have two three-month periods a year when much of the snow will disappear, and we will be in the middle of one of them. It will not be bad. Of course we will have to get the jump on our little red minded brothers. That will not be easy."

"Oh, don't hurry about that. They have one good idea. I would kind of like to have a mate by evening. Do you have any ideas?"

"I have an idea about what your idea is. But what is that look on your face? If it's a smile, it surely has some odd overtones. Violet, don't look at me like that. I can't get married. Violet—I have my work to do."

"Your work is back in New York under quite a few feet of snow. Think how deep it'll be by morning. And just remember, it will be nearly ninety thousand years before you can get back to it. That's a long time to be a bachelor."

"Yes, that's a long time, Violet—I never thought about it that way."

"Which would you rather have, me or the sadist group?"

"I don't know, Violet. There's a lot to be said against both of you. Oh, I didn't mean that quite the way it sounded. I would prefer you immeasurably to the sadist group. But I have a stubborn streak. I will not be forced by these jokers."

"Couldn't you be stubborn about something else? There will be much you can be stubborn about under these new circumstances."

"I will be stubborn about this. Maybe it is only about fifteen above zero, maybe there are only seven or ten inches of snow. And even though it will moderate within ten days it will be bitter tonight. Be a good girl, get your bolo, and see how much wood you can cut."

"I had a date tonight for the opening of 'Pink Snow'. Now I don't believe there will be any opening, and my boyfriend has probably frozen to death."

They worked hard as the afternoon wore on. Commander Andreyev kept buzzing around them; and, though he was insulting, yet he seemed to want their company.

"Professor Gilluly, you are high in the confidence of Dr. Eimer. Has he any particular ideas of governing this colony?"

"None that I know of. Ask him. Here he comes."

"No. None, Andy—we figured it would take care of itself."

"And now providently we have taken that worry from you."

"There was no worry, and you have taken nothing from us."

"I am the commander of the world," said Andreyev.

"You said that before."

"My superiors will all be dead in hours or days. There will be no one to give me orders." He said this last wistfully.

"Do you need someone to give you orders?"

"No. No. Of course not. Now I shall give the orders." And he went away.

* * * *

But in less than an hour he was back.

"Do you think, Dr. Eimer, that it is snowing harder in Moscow than in New York?"

"Of course it is. That is in line with my predictions. Is it not in line with yours?"

"Certainly. But I only wondered…"

"What?"

"I wondered if it were possible for someone to be making it snow very hard in my country?"

"What are you talking about? How could anyone be making it snow? You have been studying the coming glaciation for twenty years. What is the matter with you now?"

"It is nothing, nothing at all. It is just something I picked up on the radio a moment ago. You understand there is a great deal of panic in the world, and many things are being said that in normal times would not seem normal. It is just something I heard on the radio."

He went away. And the professors, doctors, and assorted persons worked very hard until they had attained the means and assurance of shelter and heat for the night. Then they rested.

"I always thought you were all crazy," said Violet, "but you paid well—so I worked for you. But how did you know it was going to get cold? What makes an ice age?"

"There's a lot of things that can do it, Violet. It only takes a little change. Between freezing and melting there is only a fraction of a degree, and if it is worldwide that is all that is needed. There is a solar variable cycle involved here, and an oxygen carbon-dioxide balance or unbalance: there is a cloud envelope disparity and a change of worldwide air flow. But that is just a fancy way of saying it, Violet. The straight fact is that every now and then it just plain gets cold."

* * * *

About dark, commander Andreyev came to them again.

"I extend the hand of friendship," said Andreyev.

"Good for you, Andy."

"My remarks earlier today were intemperate and ill-advised."

"Indeed they were. But how did you come to realize it?"

"I propose that we join our forces."

"I propose that we leave things unjoined. We should gradually learn to get along."

"I propose that you reign as supreme commander, Dr. Eimer."

"I propose that you get over your nonsense, whatever it is."

"I am putting all my forces at your disposal, everything, even my sadist group—they are yours. Say the word. Is there anyone you want tortured or intimidated. They are avid to do it."

"There is nobody. But please explain the change."

"Dr. Eimer, if you were accustomed to obeying orders and believed it right to do so, should you not obey a final order—even though it were unenforceable on you?"

"I think so."

"It is an order I received, perhaps the last order that will come over the air. There have been all-channel and all languages broadcasts. I cannot disobey an order. It is to all our commanders and agents everywhere in the world."

"And what is the order?"

"It is that we surrender unconditionally to you."

"What is there left to surrender? And why have they done it?"

"They seem to believe in my country, even the leaders—oh, I don't know how to say what they believe in my country!"

* * * *

For if it was snowing in Washington and New York, and in the tropics, it was snowing doubly in Moscow—an odd quirk of the new glaciation that had been predicted by both Dr. Eimer and Commander Andreyev working independently on two different continents.

By noon eastern time, when white night had already descended on the Russias, the mysterious urgent pleas had come to a heart-rending climax.

By cable and broadcast came the notes.

"The launchings were unauthorized," said the first note.

"The launchings were in error. We request that you stop the snow until negotiations can be resumed," said the second.

"Urgent, repeat, urgent, that snow be stopped," said the third.

It was a puzzled President and staff that read the cables, and a mystified public that heard the broadcasts. They did not immediately realize that Moscow believed the incredible snow was an American secret weapon, unleashed in retaliation of the missile launchings and destruction of the American bases.

The notes became pleading: "Government being completely redesigned on more amenable lines. Request patience and understanding. Urgent snow be stopped. It is now more than four meters. Advise surrender terms. Cessation of nivalation critical."

"It is hardly less critical here," said the President. "Nine feet is no light snow, and I doubt if it can be stopped by either act of Congress or executive directive. I could give a lot of orders, but what good would it do? Nobody is going anywhere."

By the time of the Washington dusk, which was only a grey overlay of the blurred white, Moscow was buried under twenty-six feet of snow, and there was two-thirds as much over most of America.

* * * *

Down in the Padiwire Valley on the equator Dr. Eimer, Professors Schubert and Gilluly and some others went with abdicated Commander Andreyev to his tent to hear the last of the broadcasts.

"Abject surrender. Request for the love of God you stop snow." And the last message was only a broken particle of phrase: "Milocerd!"

Mercy!

SODOM AND GOMORRAH, TEXAS

Manuel shouldn't have been employed as a census taker. He wasn't qualified. He couldn't read a map. He didn't know what a map was. He only grinned when they told him that North was at the top.

He knew better.

But he did write a nice round hand, like a boy's hand. He knew Spanish, and enough English. For the sector that was assigned to him he would not need a map. He knew it better than anyone else, certainly better than any mapmaker. Besides, he was poor and needed the money.

They instructed him and sent him out. Or they thought that they had instructed him. They couldn't be sure.

"Count everyone? All right. Fill in everyone? I need more papers."

"We will give you more if you need more. But there aren't so many in your sector."

"Lots of them. *Lobos, tejones, zorros*, even people."

"Only the *people*, Manuel! Do not take the animals. How would you write up the animals? They have no names."

"Oh, yes. All have names. Might as well take them all."

"Only people, Manuel."

"*Mulos?*"

"No."

"*Conejos?*"

"No, Manuel, no. Only the people."

"No trouble. Might as well take them all."

"Only people—God give me strength!—only people, Manuel."

"How about little people?"

"Children, yes. That has been explained to you."

"*Little* people. Not children, little people."

"If they are people, take them."

"How big they have to be?"

"It doesn't make any difference how big they are. If they are people, take them."

That is where the damage was done.

The official had given a snap judgement, and it led to disaster. It was not his fault. The instructions are not clear. Nowhere in all the verbiage does it say how big they have to be to be counted as people.

* * * *

Manuel took Mula and went to work. His sector was the Santa Magdalena, a scrap of bald-headed and desolate mountains, steep but not high, and so torrid in the afternoons that it was said that the old lava sometimes began to writhe and flow again from the sun's heat alone.

In the center valley there were five thousand acres of slag and vitrified rock from some forgotten old blast that had melted the hills and destroyed their mantle, reducing all to a terrible flatness. This was called Sodom. It was strewn with low-lying ghosts as of people and objects, formed when the granite bubbled like water.

Away from the dead center the ravines were body-deep in chaparral, and the hillsides stood gray-green with old cactus. The stunted trees were lower than the giant bushes and yucca.

Manuel went with Mula, a round easy man and a sparse gaunt mule. Mula was a mule, but there were other inhabitants of the Santa Magdalena of a genus less certain.

Yet even about Mula there was an oddity in her ancestry. Her paternal grandfather had been a goat. Manuel once told Mr. Marshal about this, but Mr. Marshal had not accepted it.

"She is a mule. Therefore, her father was a jack. Therefore his father was also a jack, a donkey. It could not be any other way."

Manuel often wondered about that, for he had raised the whole strain of animals, and he remembered who had been with whom.

"A donkey! A jack! Two feet tall and with a beard and horns. I always thought that he was a goat."

Manuel and Mula stopped at noon on Lost Soul Creek. There would be no travel in the hot afternoon. But Manuel had a job to do, and he did it. He took the forms from one of the packs that he had unslung from Mula, and counted out nine of them. He wrote down all the data on nine people. He knew all there was to know about them, their nativities and their antecedents. He knew that there were only nine regular people in the nine hundred square miles of the Santa Magdalena.

But he was systematic, so he checked the list over again and again. There seemed to be somebody missing. Oh, yes, himself. He got another form and filled out all the data on himself.

Now, in one way of looking at it, his part in the census was finished. If only he had looked at it that way, he would have saved worry and trouble for everyone, and also ten thousand lives. But the instructions they had given him were ambiguous, for all that they had tried to make them clear.

So very early the next morning he rose and cooked beans, and said, "Might as well take them all."

He called Mula from the thorn patch where she was grazing, gave her salt and loaded her again. Then they went to take the rest of the census, but in fear. There was a clear duty to get the job done, but there was also a dread of it that his superiors did not understand. There was reason also why Mula was loaded so she could hardly walk with packs of census forms.

Manuel prayed out loud as they climbed the purgatorial scarp above Lost Souls Creek, *"ruega por nosotros pecadores ahora—"* the very gulches stood angry and stark in the early morning—*"y en la hora de neustra muerte."*

* * * *

Three days later an incredible dwarf staggered into the outskirts of High Plains, Texas, followed by a dying wolf-sized animal that did not look like a wolf.

A lady called the police to save the pair from rock-throwing kids who might have killed them, and the two as yet unclassified things were taken to the station house.

The dwarf was three foot high, a skeleton stretched over with brown-burnt leather. The other was an un-canine looking dog-sized beast, so full of burrs and thorns that it might have been a porcupine. It was a nightmare replica of a shrunken mule.

The midget was mad. The animal had more presence of mind: she lay down quietly and died, which was the best she could do, considering the state that she was in.

"Who is census chief now?" asked the mad midget. "Is Mr. Marshal's boy the census chief?"

"Mr. Marshal is, yes. Who are you? How do you know Marshal? And what is that which you are pulling out of your pants, if they are pants?"

"Census list. Names of everybody in the Santa Magdalena. I had to steal it."

"It looks like microfilm, the writing is so small. And the roll goes on and on. There must be a million names here."

"Little bit more, little bit more. I get two bits a name."

They got Marshal there. He was very busy, but he came. He had been given a deadline by the mayor and the citizen's group. He had to produce a population of ten thousand people for High Plains, Texas; and this was difficult, for there weren't that many people in the town. He had been working hard on it, though; but he came when the police called him.

"You Marshal's little boy? You look just like your father," said the midget.

"That voice, I should know that voice even if it's cracked to pieces. That has to be Manuel's voice."

"Sure, I'm Manuel. Just like I left, thirty-five years ago."

"You can't be Manuel, shrunk three feet and two hundred pounds and aged a million."

"You look here at my census slip. It says I'm Manuel. And here are nine more of the regular people, and one million of the little people. I couldn't get them on the right forms, though. I had to steal their list."

"You can't be Manuel," said Marshal.

"He can't be Manuel," said the big policemen and the little policeman.

"Maybe not, then," the dwarf conceded. "I thought I was, but I wasn't sure. Who am I then? Let's look at the other papers and see which one I am."

"No, you can't be any of them either, Manuel. And you surely can't be Manuel."

"Give him a name anyhow and get him counted. We got to get to that ten thousand mark."

"Tell us what happened, Manuel—if you are. Which you aren't. But tell us."

"After I counted the regular people I went to count the little people. I took a spade and spaded off the top of their town to get in. But they put an *encanto* on me, and made me and Mula run a treadmill for thirty-five years."

"Where was this?"

"At the little people town. Nuevo Danae. But after thirty-five years the *encanto* wore off and Mula and I stole the list of names and ran away."

"But where did you really get this list of so many names written so small?"

"Suffering saddle sores, Marshal, don't ask the little bug so many questions. You got a million names in your hand. Certify them! Send them in! There's enough of us here right now. We declare that place annexed forthwith. This will make High Plains the biggest town in the whole state of Texas."

* * * *

So Marshal certified them and sent them into Washington. This gave High Plains the largest percentage increase of any city in the nation, but it was challenged. There were some soreheads in Houston who said that it wasn't possible. They said High Plains had nowhere near that many people and there must have been a miscount.

And in the days that the argument was going on, they cleaned up and fed Manuel, if it were he, and tried to get from him a cogent story.

"How do you know it was thirty-five years you were on the treadmill, Manuel?"

"Well, it seemed like thirty-five years."

"It could have only been about three days."

"Then how come I'm so old?"

"We don't know that, Manuel, we sure don't know that. How big were these people?"

"Who knows? A finger long, maybe two?"

"And what is their town?"

"It is an old prairie-dog town that they fixed up. You have to dig down with a spade to get to the streets."

"Maybe they were really all prairie dogs, Manuel. Maybe the heat got you and you only dreamed that they were little people."

"Prairie dogs can't write as good as on that list. Prairie dogs can't write hardly at all."

"That's true. The list is hard to explain. And such odd names on it too."

"Where is Mula? I don't see Mula since I came back."

"Mula just lay down and died, Manuel."

"Gave me the slip. Why didn't I think of that? Well, I'll do it too. I'm too worn out for anything else."

"Before you do, Manuel, just a couple of last questions."

"Make them real fast then. I'm on my way."

"Did you know these little people were there before?"

"Oh, sure. There a long time."

"Did anybody else ever see them?"

"Oh, sure. Everybody in the Santa Magdalena see them. Eight, nine people see them."

"And Manuel, how do we get to the place? Can you show us on a map?"

Manuel made a grimace, and died quietly as Mula had done. He didn't understand those maps at all, and took the easy way out.

They buried him, not knowing for sure whether he was Manuel come back, or what he was.

There wasn't much of him to bury.

* * * *

It was the same night, very late and after he had been asleep, that Marshal was awakened by the ring of an authoritative voice. He was being harangued by a four-inch tall man on his bedside table, a man of dominating presence and acid voice.

"Come out of that cot, you clown! Give me your name and station!"

"I'm Marshal, and I suspect that you are a late pig sandwich, or caused by one. I shouldn't eat so late."

"Say 'sir' when you reply to me. I am no pig sandwich and I do not commonly call on fools. Get on your feet, you clod."

And wonderingly Marshal did.

"I want the list that was stolen. Don't gape! Get it!"

"What list?"

"Don't stall, don't stutter. Get me our tax list that was stolen. It isn't words that I want from you."

"Listen, you cicada, I'll take you and—"

"You will not. You will notice that you are paralyzed from the neck down. I suspect that you were always so from there up. Where is the list?"

"S-sent it to Washington."

"You bug-eyed behemoth! Do you realize what a trip that will be? You grandfather of inanities, it will be a pleasure to destroy you!"

"I don't know what you are, or if you are really. I don't believe that you even belong on the world."

"Not belong on the world! We own the world. We can show written title to the world. Can you?"

"I doubt it. Where did you get the title?"

"None of your business. I'd rather not say. Oh, well, we got it from a promoter of sorts. A con man, really. I'll have to admit that we were taken, but we were in a spot and needed a world. He said that the larger bifurcates were too stupid to be a nuisance. We should have known that the stupider a creature, the more of a nuisance it is."

"I had about decided the same thing about the smaller a creature. We may have to fumigate that old mountain mess."

"Oh, you can't harm us. We're too powerful. But we can obliterate you in an instant."

"Hah!"

"Say 'Hah, *sir*' when you address me. Do you know the place in the mountain that is called Sodom?"

"I know the place. It was caused by a large meteor."

"It was caused by one of these."

What he held up was the size of a grain of sand. Marshal could not see it in detail.

"There was another city of you bug-eyed beasts there," said the small martinet. "You wouldn't know about it. It's been a few hundred years. We decided it was too close. Now I have decided that you are too close."

"A thing that size couldn't crack a walnut."

"You floundering fop, it will blast this town flat!"

"What will happen to you?"

"Nothing. I don't even blink for things like that."

"How do you trigger it off."

"You gaping goof, I don't have time to explain that to you. I have to get to Washington."

It may be that Marshal did not believe himself quite awake. He certainly did not take the threat seriously enough. For the little man did trigger it off.

* * * *

When the final count was in, High Plains did not have the highest percentage gain in population in the nation. Actually it showed the sharpest decline, from 7313 to nothing.

They were going to make a forest preserve out of the place, except that it has no trees worthy of the name. Now it is proposed to make it the Sodom and Gomorrah State Park from the two mysterious scenes of desolation there, just seven miles apart.

It is an interesting place, as wild a region as you will ever find, and is recommended for the man who has seen everything.

THROUGH OTHER EYES

I

"I don't think I can stand the dawn of another Great Day," said Smirnov. "It always seems a muggy morning, a rainy afternoon and a dismal evening. You remember the Recapitulation Correlator?"

"Known popularly as the Tune Machine. But, Gregory, that was and is a success. All three of them are in constant use, and they will construct at least one more a decade. They are invaluable."

"Yes. It was a dismal success. It has turned my whole life gray. You remember our trial run, the recapitulation of the Battle of Hastings?"

"It was a depressing three years we spent there. But how were we to know it was such a small affair—covering less than five acres of that damnable field and lasting less than twenty minutes? And how were we to know that an error of four years had been made in history even as recent as that? Yes, we scanned many depressing days and many muddy fields in that area before we recreated it."

"And our qualified success at catching the wit of Voltaire at first hand?"

"Gad! That cackle! There can never be anything new in nausea to one who has sickened of that. What a perverted old woman he was!"

"And Nell Guinn?"

"There is no accounting for the taste of a king. What a completely tasteless morsel!"

"And the crowning of Charlemagne?"

"The king of chilblains. If you wanted a fire, you carried it with you in a basket. That was the coldest Christmas I ever knew. But the mead seemed to warm them; and we were the only ones present who could not touch it or taste it."

"And when we went further back and heard the wonderful words of the divine poetess Sappho."

"Yes, she had just decided that she would have her favorite cat spayed. We listened to her for three days and she talked of nothing else. How fortunate the world is that so few of her words have survived."

"And watching the great Pythagoras at work."

"And the long days he spent on that little surveying problem. How one longed to hand him a slide rule through the barrier and explain its workings."

"And our eavesdropping on the great lovers Tristram and Isolde."

"And him spending a whole afternoon trying to tune that cursed harp with a penny whistle. And she could talk of nothing but the bear grease she used on her hair, and how it was nothing like the bear grease back home. But she was a cute little lard barrel, quite the cutest we found for several centuries in either direction. One wouldn't be able to get one's arms all the way around her; but I can understand how, to one of that era and region, it would be fun trying."

"Ah yes. Smelled like a cinnamon cookie, didn't she? And you recall Lancelot?"

"Always had a bad back that wouldn't let him ride. And that trick elbow and the old groin wound. He spent more time on the rubbing table than any athlete I ever heard of. If I had a high-priced quarterback who was never ready to play, I'd sure find a way of breaking his contract. No use keeping him on the squad just to read his ten-year-old press clippings. Any farm boy could have pulled him off his nag and stomped him into the dirt."

"I wasn't too happy about Aristotle the day we caught him. That barbarous north-coast Greek of his! Three hours he had them all busy combing his beard. And his discourse on the Beard in Essential and the Beard in Existential, did you follow that?"

"No, to tell the truth I didn't. I guess it was pretty profound."

They were silent and sad for a while, as are men who have lost much.

"The machine was a success," said Smirnov at last, "and yet the high excitement of it died dismally for us."

"The excitement is in the discovery of the machine," said Cogsworth. "It is never in what the machine discovers."

"And this new one of yours," said Smirnov, "I hardly want to see you put it into operation. I am sure it will be a shattering disappointment to you."

"I am sure of it also. And yet it is greater than the other. I am as excited as a boy."

"You were a boy before, but you will never be again. I should think it would have aged you enough, and I cannot see what fascination this new one will have for you. At least the other recaptured the past. This will permit you to see only the present."

"Yes, but through other eyes."

"One pair of eyes is enough. I do not see any advantage at all except the novelty. I am afraid that this will be only a gadget."

"No. Believe me, Smirnov, it will be more than that. It may not even be the same world when viewed through different eyes. I believe that what we regard as one may actually be several billion different universes, each made only for the eyes of the one who sees it."

II

The Cerebral Scanner, newly completed by Charles Cogsworth, was not an intricate machine. It was a small but ingenious amplifying device, or battery of amplifiers, designed for the synchronous—perhaps "sympathetic" would be a better word—coupling of two very intricate machines: two human brains. It was an amplifier only. A subliminal coupling, or the possibility of it, was already assumed by the inventor. Less than a score of key aspects needed emphasizing for the whole thing to come to life.

Here the only concern was with the convoluted cortex of the brain itself, that house of consciousness and terminal of the senses, and with the quasi-electrical impulses which are the indicators of its activity. It had been a long-held opinion of Cogsworth that, by the proper amplification of a near score of these impulses in one brain, a transmission could be effected to another so completely that one man might for an instant see with the eyes of another—also see inwardly with that man's eyes, have the same imaginings and daydreams, perceive the same universe as the other perceived. And it would not be the same universe as the seeking man knew.

The Scanner had been completed, as had a compilation of the dossiers of seven different brains: a collection of intricate brain-wave data as to frequency, impulse, flux and field, and Lyall-wave patterns of the seven cerebrums which Cogsworth would try to couple with his own.

The seven were those of Gregory Smirnov, his colleague and counselor in so many things; of Gaetan Balbo, the cosmopolitan and supra-national head of the Institute; of Theodore Grammont, the theoretical mathematician; of E. E. Euler, the many-tentacled executive; of Karl Kleber, the extraordinary psychologist; of Edmond Guillames, the skeptic and bloodless critic; and of Valery Mok, a lady of beauty and charm whom Cogsworth had despaired of ever understanding by ordinary means.

This idea of his—to enter into the mind of another, to peer from behind another's eyes into a world that could not be the same—this idea had been with him all his life. He recalled how it had first come down on him in all its strength when he was quite small.

"It may be that I am the only one who sees the sky black at night and the stars white," he had said to himself, "and everybody else sees the sky white and the stars shining black. And I say the sky is black, and they say the sky is black; but when they say black they mean white."

Or: "I may be the only one who can see the outside of a cow, and everybody else sees it inside out. And I say that it is the outside, and they say that it is the outside; but when they say outside they mean inside."

Or: "It may be that all the boys I see look like girls to everyone else, and all the girls look like boys. And I say 'That is a girl,' and they say 'That is a girl'; only when they say a girl they mean a boy."

And then had come the terrifying thought: "What if I am a girl to everyone except me?"

This did not seem very intelligent to him even when he was small, and yet it became an obsession to him.

"What if to a dog all dogs look like men and all men look like dogs? And what if a dog looks at me and thinks that I am a dog and he is a boy?"

And this was followed once by the shattering afterthought: "And what if the dog is right?

"What if a fish looks up at a bird and a bird looks down at a fish? And the fish thinks that he is the bird and the bird is the fish, and that he is looking down on the bird that is really a fish, and the air is water and the water is air?"

"What if, when a bird eats a worm, the worm thinks he is the bird and the bird is the worm? And that his outside is his inside, and that the bird's inside is his outside? And that he has eaten the bird instead of the bird eating him?"

This was illogical. But how does one know that a worm is not illogical? He has much to make him illogical.

And as he grew older Charles Cogsworth came on many signs that the world he saw was not the world that others saw. There came smaller but persistent signs that every person lives in a different world.

It was early in the afternoon, but Charles Cogsworth sat in darkness. Gregory Smirnov had gone for a walk in the country as he said that he would. He was the only other one who knew that the experiment was being made. He is the only one who would have agreed to the experiment, though the others had permitted their brain-wave dossiers to be compiled on another pretext.

All beginnings come quietly, and this one was a total success. The sensation of seeing with the eyes of another is new and glorious, though the full recognition of it comes slowly.

"He is a greater man than I," said Cogsworth. "I have often suspected it. He has a placidity which I do not own, though he has not my fever. And he lives in a better world."

It was a better world, greater in scope and more exciting in detail.

"Who would have thought of giving such a color to grass, if it is grass? It is what he calls grass, but it is not what I call grass. I wonder I should ever be content to see it as I saw it. It is a finer sky than I had known, and more structured hills. The old bones of them stand out for him as they do not for me, and he knows the water in their veins.

"There is a man walking toward him, and he is a grander man than I have ever seen. Yet I have also known the shadow of this man, and his name is Mr. Dottle, both to myself and to Gregory. I had thought that Dottle was a fool, but now I know that in the world of Gregory no man is a fool. I am looking through the inspired and almost divine eyes of a giant, and I am looking at a world that has not yet grown tired."

For what seemed like hours Charles Cogsworth lived in the world of Gregory Smirnov; and he found here, out of all his life, one great expectation that did not fail him.

Then, after he had rested a while, he looked at the world through the wide eyes of Gaetan Balbo.

"I am not sure that he is a greater man than I, but he is a wider man. Nor am I sure that he looks into a greater world. I would not willingly trade for his, as I would for Gregory's. Here I miss the intensity of my own. But it is fascinating, and I will enjoy returning to it again and again. And I know whose eyes these are. I am looking through the eyes of a king."

Later he saw through the eyes of Theodore Grammont, and felt a surge of pity.

"If I am blind compared to Gregory, then this man is blind compared to me. I at least know that the hills are alive; he believes them to be imperfect polyhedrons. He is in the middle of a desert and is not even able to talk to the devils who live there. He has abstracted the world and numbered it, and doesn't even know that the world is a live animal. He has built his own world of great complexity, but he cannot see the color of its flanks. This man has achieved so much only because he was denied so much at the beginning. I understand now that only the finest theory is no more than a fact gnawed on vicariously by one who has no teeth. But I will return to this world too, even though it has no body to it. I have been seeing through the eyes of a blind hermit."

Delightful and exciting as this was, yet it was tiring. Cogsworth rested for a quarter of an hour before he entered the world of E. E. Euler. When he entered it he was filled with admiration.

"An ordinary man could not look into a world like this. It would drive him out of his wits. It is almost like looking through the eyes of the Lord, who numbers all the feathers of the sparrow and every mite that nestles there. It is the interconnection vision of all the details. It appalls. It isn't an easy world even to look at. Great Mother of Ulcers! How does he stand it? Yet I see that he loves every tangled detail, the more tangled the better. This is a world in which I will be able to take only a clinical interest. Somebody must hold these reins, but happily it is not my fate. To tame this hairy old beast we live on is the doom of Euler. I look for a happier doom."

He had been looking through the eyes of a general.

The attempt to see into the world of Karl Kleber was almost a total failure. The story is told of the behaviorist who would study the chimpanzee. He put the curious animal in a room alone and locked the door on it; then went to the keyhole to spy; the keyhole was completely occupied by the brown eyeball of the animal spying back at him.

Something of the sort happened here. Though Karl Kleber was unaware of the experiment, yet the seeing was in both directions. Kleber was studying Cogsworth in those moments by some quirk of circumstance. And even when Cogsworth was able to see with the eyes of Kleber, yet it was himself he was seeing.

"I am looking through the eyes of a peeper," he said. "And yet, what am I myself?"

If the world of Gregory Smirnov first entered was the grandest, so that of Edmond Guillames, which Cogsworth entered last but one, was in all ways the meanest.

It was a world seen from the inside of a bile duct. It was not a pleasant world, just as Edmond was not a pleasant man. But how could one be other than a skeptic if all his life he had seen nothing but a world of rubbery bones and bloodless flesh clothed in crippled colors and obscene forms?

"The mole of another's world would be nobler than a lion in his," said Cogsworth. "Why should one not be a critic who has so much to criticize? Why should one not be an unbeliever when faced with the dilemma that this unsavory world was either made by God or hatched by a cross-eyed ostrich? I have looked through the eyes of a fool into a fools' world."

As Cogsworth rested again he said, "I have seen the world through the eyes of a giant, of a king, of a blind hermit, of a general, of a peeping tom, of a fool. There is nothing left but to see it through the eyes of an angel."

Valery Mok may or may not have been an angel. She was a beautiful woman, and angels, in the older and more authentic iconography, were rather stern men with shaggy pinions.

Valery wore a look of eternal amusement, and was the embodiment of all charm and delight, at least to Charles Cogsworth. He believed her to be of high wit. Yet, if driven into a corner, he would have been unable to recall one witty thing she had ever said. He regarded her as of perfect kindness, and she was more or less on the agreeable side. Yet, Smirnov had put it, she was not ordinarily regarded as extraordinary.

It was only quite lately that Cogsworth was sure that it was love he felt for her rather than bafflement. And, as he had despaired of ever understanding her by regular means, though everyone else understood her easily enough in as much as mattered, he would now use irregular means for his understanding.

He looked at the world through the eyes of Valery Mok, saying, "I will see the world through the eyes of an angel."

A change came over him as he looked, and it was not a pleasant change. He looked through her eyes for quite a while—not, perhaps, as long as he had looked through the eyes of Gregory—yet for a long time, unable to tear himself away.

He shuddered and trembled and shrank back into himself.

Then he let it alone, and buried his face in his arms.

"I have looked at the world through the eyes of a pig," he said.

III

Charles Cogsworth spent six weeks in a sanatorium, which, however, was not called that. He had given the world his second great invention, and its completion had totally exhausted him. As in many such mercurial temperaments, the exaltation of discovery had been followed by an interlude of deep despondency on its completion.

Yet he was of fundamentally sound constitution and he had the best of care. But when he recovered it was not into his old self. He now had a sort of irony smiling resignation that was new to him. It was though he had discovered a new and more bitter world for himself in looking into the worlds of others.

Of his old intimates only Gregory Smirnov was still close to him.

"I can guess the trouble, Charles," said Gregory. "I rather feared this would happen. In fact I advised against her being one of the subjects of the experiment. It is simply that you know very little about women."

"I have read all the prescribed texts, Gregory. I took a six-week seminar under Zamenoff. I am acquainted with almost the entire body of the work of Bopp concerning women. I have spent nearly as many years as you in the world, and I generally go about with my eyes open. I surely understand as much as is understandable about them."

"No. They are not your proper field. I could have predicted what has shocked you. You had not understood that women are so much more sensuous than men. But it would be better if you explained just what it was that shocked you."

"I had thought that Valery was an angel. It is simply that it is a shock to find that she is a pig."

"I doubt if you understand pigs any better than you understand women. I myself, only two days ago, had a pig's-eye view of the world, and that with your own Cerebral Scanner. I have been doing considerable work with it in the several weeks that you have been laid up. There is nothing in the pig's-eye world that would shock even the most fastidious. It is a dreamy world of all-encompassing placidity, almost entirely divorced from passion. It's a gray shadowy world with very little of the unpleasant. I had never before known how wonderful is the feel of simple sunlight and of cool earth. Yet we would soon be bored with it; but the pig is not bored."

"You divert me, Gregory, but you do not touch the point of my shock. Valery is beautiful—or was to me before this. She seemed kind and serene. Always she appeared to contain a mystery that amused her vastly, and which I suspected would be the most wonderful thing in the world once I understood it."

"And her mystery is that she lives in a highly sensuous world and enjoys it with complete awareness? Is that what has shocked you?"

"You do not know the depth of it. It is ghastly. The colors of that world are of unbelievable coarseness, and the shapes reek. The smells are the worst. Do you know how a tree smells to her?"

"What kind of tree?"

"Any tree. I think it was an ordinary elm."

"The Slippery Elm has a pleasant aroma in season. The others, to me, have none."

"No. It was not. Every tree has a strong smell in her world. This was an ordinary elm tree, and it had a violent musky obscene smell that delighted her. It was so strong that it staggered. And to her the grass itself is like clumps of snakes, and the world itself is flesh. Every bush is to her a leering satyr, and she cannot help but brush into them. The rocks are spidery monsters and she loves them. She sees every cloud as a mass of twisting bodies and she is crazy to be in the middle of them. She hugged a lamp post and her heart beat like it would fight its way out of her body.

"She can smell rain at a great distance and in a foul manner, and she wants to be in the middle of it. She worships every engine as a fire monster, and she hears sounds that I thought nobody could ever hear. Do you know what worms sound like inside the earth? They're devilish, and she would writhe and eat dirt with them. She can rest her hand on a guard rail, and it is an obscene act when she does it. There is a filthiness in every color and sound and shape and smell and feel."

"And yet, Charles, she is but a slightly more than average attractive girl, given to musing, and with a love of the world and a closeness to it that most of us have lost. She has a keen awareness of reality and of the grotesqueness that is its main mark. You yourself do not have this deeply; and when you encounter it in its full strength, it shocks you."

"You mean that is normal?"

"There is no normal. There are only differences. When you moved into our several worlds they did not shock you to the same extent, for most of the corners are worn off our worlds. But to move into a pristine universe is more of a difference than you were prepared for."

"I cannot believe that that is all it is."

Charles Cogsworth would not answer the letters of Valery Mok, nor would he see her. Yet her letters were amusing and kind, and carried a trace of worry for him.

"I wonder what I smell like to her?" he asked himself. "Am I like an elm tree, or a worm in the ground? What color am I to her? Is my voice obscene? She says she misses the sound of my voice. It should be possible to undo this. Am I also to her like a column of snakes or a congeries of spiders?"

For he wasn't well yet from what he had seen.

But he did go back to work, and nibbled at the edges of mystery with his fantastic device. He even looked into the worlds of other women. It was as Smirnov had said: they were more sensuous than men but none of them to the shocking degree of Valery.

He saw with the eyes of other men. And of animals: the soft pleasure of the fox devouring a ground squirrel, the bloody anger of a lamb furious after milk, the crude arrogance of the horse, the intelligent tolerance of the mule, the voraciousness of the cow, the miserliness of the squirrel, the sullen passion of the catfish. Nothing was quite as might have been expected.

He learned the jealousy and hatred that beautiful women hold against the ugly, the untarnished evil of small children, the diabolic possession of adolescents. He even, by accident, saw the world through the fleshless eyes of a poltergeist, and through the eyes of creatures that he could not identify at all. He found nobility in places that almost balanced the pervading baseness.

But mostly he loved to see the world through the eyes of his friend Gregory Smirnov, for there is a grandeur on everything when seen through a giant's eyes.

And one day he saw Valery Mok through the eyes of Smirnov when they met accidentally. Something of his old feeling came back to him, and something that even surpassed his former regard. She was here magnificent, as was everything in that world. And there had to be a common ground between that wonderful world with her in it and the hideous world seen through her own eyes.

"I am wrong somewhere," said Cogsworth. "It is because I do not understand enough. I will go and see her."

But instead she came to see him.

She burst in on him furiously one day.

"You are a stick. You are a stick with no blood in it. You are a pig made out of sticks. You live with dead people Charles. You make everything dead. You are abominable."

"I a pig, Valery? Possibly. But I never saw a pig made out of sticks."

"Then see yourself. That is what you are."

"Tell me what this is about."

"It is about you. You are a pig made out of sticks, Charles. Gregory Smirnov let me use your machine. I saw the world the way you see it. I saw it with a dead man's eyes. You don't even know that the grass is alive. You think it's only grass."

"I also saw the world with your eyes, Valery."

"Oh, is that what's been bothering you? Well, I hope it livened you up a little. It's a livelier world than yours."

"More pungent, at least."

"Lord, I should hope so. I don't think you even have a nose. I don't think you have any eyes. You can look at a hill and your heart doesn't even skip a beat. You don't even tingle when you walk over a field."

"You see grass like clumps of snakes."

"That's better than not even seeing it alive."

"You see rocks like big spiders."

"That's better than just seeing them like rocks. I love snakes and spiders. You can watch a bird fly by and not even hear the stuff gurgling in its stomach. How can you be so dead? And I always liked you so much. But I didn't know you were dead like that."

"How can one love snakes and spiders?"

"How can one not love anything? It's even hard not to love you, even if you don't have any blood in you. By the way, what gave you the idea that blood was that dumb color? Don't you even know that blood is red?"

"I see it red."

"You don't see it red. You just call it red. That sill color isn't red. What I call red is red."

And he knew that she was right.

And after all, how can one not love anything? Especially when it becomes beautiful when angry, and when it is so much alive that it tends to shock by its intense awareness those who are partly dead.

Now Charles Cogsworth was a scientific man, and he believed that there are no insoluble problems. He solved this one too; for he had found that Valery was a low-flying bird, and he began to understand what was gurgling inside her.

And he solved it happily.

* * * *

He is working on a Correlator for his Scanner now. When this is perfected, it will be safe to give the device to the public. You will be able to get the combination in about three years at approximately the price of a medium-sized new car. And if you will wait another year, you may be able to get one of the used ones reasonably.

The Correlator is designed to minimize and condition the initial view of the world seen through other eyes, to soften the shock of understanding others.

Misunderstandings can be agreeable. But there is something shattering about sudden perfect understanding.

THE WEIRDEST WORLD

I

As I am now utterly without hope, lost to my mission and lost in the sight of my crew, I will record what petty thoughts I may have for what benefit they may give some other starfarer. Nine long days of bickering! But the decision is sure. The crew will maroon me. I have lost all control over them.

Who would have believed that I would show such weakness when crossing the barrier? By all tests I should have been the strongest. But the final test was the event itself. I failed.

I only hope that it is a pleasant and habitable planet where they put me down...

Later. They have decided. I am no longer the captain even in name. But they have compassion on me. They will do what they can for my comfort. I believe that they have already selected my desert island, so to speak, an out-of-the-way globe where they will leave me to die. I will hope for the best. I no longer have any voice in their councils...

Later. I will be put down with only the basic survival kit: the ejection mortar and sphere for my last testament to be orbited into the Galactic drift; a small cosmoscope so that I will at least have my bearings; one change of blood; an abridged universal language correlator; a compendium of the one thousand philosophic questions yet unsolved to exercise my mind; a small vial of bug-kill.

Later. It has been selected. But my mind has grown so demoralized that I do not even recognize the system, though once this particular region was my specialty. The globe will be habitable. There will be breathable atmosphere which will allow me to dispense with much bothersome equipment. Here the filler used is nitrogen, yet it will not matter. I have breathed nitrogen before. There will be water, much of it saline, but sufficient quantities of sweet. Food will be no problem; before being marooned, I will receive injections that should last me for the rest of my probably short life. Gravity will be within the range of my constitution.

What will be lacking? Nothing, but the companionship of my own kind, which is everything.

What a terrible thing it is to be marooned!

One of my teachers used to say that the only unforgivable sin in the universe is ineptitude. That I should be the first to succumb to space-ineptitude and be an awkward burden on the rest of them! But it would be disastrous for them to try to travel any longer with a sick man, particularly as their nominal leader. I would be a shadow over them. I hold them no rancor.

It will be today…

Later. I am here. I have no real interest in defining where "here" is, though I have my cosmoscope and could easily determine it. I was anesthetized a few hours before, and put down here in my sleep. The blasted half-acre of their landing is near. No other trace of them is left.

Yet it is a good choice and not greatly unlike home. It is the nearest resemblance I have seen on the entire voyage, which is to say that the pseudodendrons are enough like trees to remind me of trees, the herbage near enough to grass to satisfy one who had never known real grass. It is a green, somewhat waterlogged land of pleasant temperature.

The only inhabitants I have encountered are a preoccupied race of hump-backed browsers who pay me scant notice. They are quadruped and myopic, and spend nearly their entire time at feeding. It may be that I am invisible to them. Yet they hear my voice and shy away somewhat from it. I am able to communicate with them only poorly. Their only vocalization is a sort of vibrant windy roar, but when I answer in kind they appear more puzzled than communicative.

They have this peculiarity: when they come to an obstacle of terrain or thicket, they either go laboriously around it or force their way through it. It does not seem to occur to them to fly over it: They are as gravity-bound as a newborn baby.

What air-traveling creatures I have met are of a considerably smaller size. They are more vocal than the myopic quadrupeds, and I have had some success in conversing with them, but my results still await a more leisurely semantic interpretation. Such communications of theirs as I have analyzed are quite commonplace. They have no real philosophy and are singularly lacking in aspiration; they are almost total extroverts and have no more than the rudiments of introspection.

Yet they have managed to tell me some amusing anecdotes. They are quite good natured, though moronic.

They say that neither they nor the myopic quadrupeds are the dominant race here, but rather a large grublike creature lacking a complete outer covering. From what they are able to convey of this breed, it is a nightmarish kind of creation. One of the flyers even told me that the giant grubs travel upright on a bifurcated tail, but that is difficult to credit. Besides, I believe that humor is at least a minor component of the mentality of my airy friends. I will call them birds, though they are but a sorry caricature of the birds at home…

Later. I am being hunted. I am being hunted by the giant grubs. Doubling back, I have seen them on my trail, examining it with great curiosity.

The birds had given me a very inadequate idea of these. They are indeed unfinished—they do lack a complete outer covering. Despite their giant size, I am convinced that they are grubs, living under rocks and in masses of rotten wood. Nothing in nature gives the impression of so lacking an outer covering as the grub, that obese, unfinished worm. There are, however, simple bipeds. They are wrapped in a cocoon which they seem never to have shed, as though their emergence from the larval state were incomplete. It is a loose artificial sheath covering the central portion of the corpus. They seem unable to divest themselves of it, though it is definitely not a part of the body. When I have analyzed their minds, I will know the reason for their carrying it. Now I can only conjecture. It would seem a compulsion, some psychological bond that dooms them in their apparent adult state to carry their cocoons with them.

Later. I am captured by three of the giant grubs. I had barely time to swallow my communication sphere. They pinned me down and beat me with sticks. I was taken by surprise and was not momentarily able to solve their language, though it came to me after a short interval. It was discordant and vocal and entirely gravity-bound, by which I mean that its thoughts were chained to its words. There seemed nothing in them above the vocal. In this the giant grubs were less than the birds, even though they had a practical power and cogency that the birds lacked.

"What'll we do with the blob?" asked one.

"Hy," said the second, "you hit it on that end and I'll hit it on this. We don't know which end is the head."

"Let's try it for bait," said the third. "Catfish might go for it."

"We could keep it alive till we're ready to use it. Then it would stay fresh."

"No, let's kill it. It doesn't look too fresh, even the way it is."

"Gentlemen, you are making a mistake," I said. "I have done nothing to merit death. And I am not without talent. Besides, you have not considered the possibility that I may be forced to kill you three instead. I will not die willingly. And I will thank you to stop pounding on me with those sticks. It hurts."

I was surprised and shocked at the sound of my own voice. It was nearly as harsh as that of the grubs. But this was my first attempt at their language, and musicality does not become it.

"Hey fellows, did you hear that? Was that the blob talking? Or was one of you playing a joke? Harry? Stanley? Have you been practicing to be ventriloquists?"

"Not me."

"Not me either. It sure sounded like it was it."

"Hey blob, was that you? Can you talk, blob?"

"Certainly I can talk," I responded. "I am not an infant. Nor am I a blob. I am a creature superior to your own kind, if you are examples. Or it may be that you are only children. Perhaps you are still in the pupa stage. Tell me, is yours an early stage, or an arrested development, or are you indeed adult?"

"Hey fellows, we don't have to take that from any blob. I'll cave in his blasted head."

"That isn't its head, it's its tail."

"Gentlemen, perhaps I can set you straight," I said. "That is my tail you are thwacking with those sticks, and I am warning you to stop it. Of course I was talking with my tail. I was only doing it in imitation of you. I am new at the language and its manner of speaking. Yet it may be that I have made a grotesque mistake. Is that your heads that you are waving in the air? Well, then, I will talk with my head, if that is the custom. But I warn you again not to hit me on either end with those sticks."

"Hey, fellows, I bet we could sell that thing. I bet we could sell it to Billy Wilkins for his Reptile Farm."

"How would we get it there?"

"Make it walk. Hey blob, can you walk?"

"I can travel, certainly, but I would not stagger along precariously on a pair of flesh stilts with my head in the air, as you do. When I travel, I do not travel upside down."

"Well, let's go then. We're going to sell you to Billy Wilkins for his Reptile Farm. If he can use a blob, he'll put you in one of the tanks with the big turtles and alligators. You think you'll like them?"

"I am lonesome in this lost world," I replied sadly, "and even the company of you peeled grubs is better than nothing. I am anxious to adopt a family and settle down here for what years of life I have left. It may be that I will find compatibility with the species you mention. I do not know what they are."

"Hey, fellows, this blob isn't a bad guy at all. I'd shake your hands, blob, if I knew where they were. Let's go to Billy Wilkins's place and sell him."

II

We traveled to Billy Wilkins's place. My friends were amazed when I took to the air and believed that I had deserted them. They had no cause to distrust me. Without them I would have had to rely on intuition to reach Billy Wilkins, and even then I would lack the proper introductions.

"Hey, Billy," said my loudest friend whose name was Cecil, "what will you give us for a blob? It flies and talks and isn't a bad fellow at all. You'd get more tourists to come to your reptile show if you had a talking blob in it. He could sing songs, and tell stories, and I bet he could play the guitar."

"Well, Cecil, I'll just give you all ten dollars for it and try to figure out what it is later. I'm a little ahead on my hunches now, so I can afford to gamble on this one. I can always pickle it and exhibit it as a genuine hippopotamus kidney."

"Thank you, Billy. Take care of yourself, blob."

"Good-bye for now, gentlemen," I said. "I would like you to visit me some evening as soon as I am acclimated to my new surroundings. I will throw a whing-ding for you—as soon as I find out what a whing-ding is."

"My God," said Billy Wilkins, "it talks, it really talks!"

"We told you it could talk and fly, Billy."

"It talks, it talks," said Billy. "Where's that blasted sign painter? Eustace, come here. We got to paint a new sign."

The turtles in the tank I was put into did have a sound basic philosophy which was absent in the walking grubs. But they were slow and lacking inner fire. They would not be obnoxious company, but neither would they give me excitement and warmth. I was really more interested in the walking grubs.

Eustace was a black grub, while the others had all been white; but like them he had no outside casing of his own, and like them he also staggered about on flesh stilts with his head in the air.

It wasn't that I was naïve or hadn't seen bipeds before. But I don't believe anyone ever becomes entirely accustomed to seeing a biped travel in its peculiar manner.

"Good afternoon, Eustace," I said pleasantly enough. The eyes of Eustace were large and white. He was a more handsome specimen than the other grubs.

"That you talking, bub? Say, you really can talk, can't you? I thought Mr. Billy was fooling. Now just hold that expression a minute and let me get it set in my mind. I can paint anything, once I get it set in my mind. What's your name, blob? Have blobs names?"

"Not in your manner. With us the name and the soul, I believe you call it, are the same thing and cannot be vocalized. I will have to adopt a name of your sort. What would be a good name?"

"Bub, I was always partial to George Albert Leroy Ellery. That was my grandfather's name."

"Should I also have a family name?"

"Sure."

"What would you suggest?"

"How about McIntosh?"

"That will be fine. I will use it."

I talked to the turtles while Eustace was painting my portrait on tent canvas.

"Is the name of this world Florida?" I asked one of them. "The road signs said Florida."

"World, world, world, water, water, water, glub, glug, glub," said one of them.

"Yes, but is this particular world we are on named Florida?"

"World, world, water, water, glub," said another.

"Eustace, I can get nothing from these fellows," I called. "Is this world named Florida?"

"Mr. George Albert, you are right in the middle of Florida, the greatest state in the universe."

"Having traveled, Eustace, I have great reservations that it is the greatest. But it is my new home and I must cultivate a loyalty to it."

I went up in a tree to give advice to two young birds trying to construct a nest. This was obviously their first venture.

"You are going about it all wrong," I told them. "First consider that this will be your home, and then consider how you can make your home most beautiful."

"This is the way they've always built them," said one of the birds.

"There must be an element of utility, yes," I told them. "But the dominant motif should be beauty. The impression of expanded vistas can be given by long low walls and parapets."

"This is the way they've always built them," said the other bird.

"Remember to embody all the new developments," I said. "Just say to yourself 'This is the newest nest in the world.' Always say that about any task you attempt. It inspires you."

"This is the way they've always built them," said the birds. "Go build your own nest."

"Mr. George Albert," called Eustace. "Mr. Billy won't like your flying around those trees. You're supposed to stay in your tank."

"I was only getting a little air and talking to the birds," I said.

"You can talk to the birds?" asked Eustace.

"Cannot anyone?"

"I can, a little," said Eustace. "I didn't know anyone else could."

But when Billy Wilkins returned and heard the report that I had been flying about, I was put in the snake house, in a cage that was tightly meshed top and sides. My cell mate was a surly python named Pete.

"See you stay on that side," said Pete. "You're too big for me to swallow. But I might try."

"There is something bothering you, Pete," I said. "You have a bad disposition. That can come only from bad digestion or a bad conscience."

"I have both," said Pete. "The first because I bolt my food. The second is because—well I forget the reason, but it's my conscience."

"Think hard, Pete," I said, "why have you a bad conscience."

"Snakes always have bad consciences. We have forgotten the crime, but we remember the guilt."

"Perhaps you should seek advice from someone, Pete."

"I kind of think it was someone's smooth advice that started us on all this. He talked the legs right off us."

Billy Wilkins came to the cage with another "man" as walking grubs call themselves.

"That it?" asked the other man. "And you say it can talk?"

"Of course I can talk," I answered for Billy Wilkins. "I have never known a creature who couldn't talk in some manner. My name is George Albert Leroy Ellery McIntosh. I don't believe that I heard yours, sir."

"Bracken. Blackjack Bracken. I was telling Billy here that if he really had a blob that could talk, that I might be able to use it in my night club. We could have you here at the Snake Ranch in the daytime for the tourists and kids. Then I could have you at the club at night. We could work out an act. Do you think you could learn to play the guitar?"

"Probably. But it would be much easier for me merely to duplicate the sound."

"But then how could you sing and make guitar noises at the same time?"

"You surely don't think that I am limited to one voice box?"

"Oh, I didn't know. What's that big metal ball you have there?"

"That's my communication sphere to record my thoughts. I would not be without it. When in danger, I swallow it. When in extreme danger, I will have to escape to a spot where I have concealed my ejection mortar, and send my sphere into the Galactic drift on a chance that it may be found."

"That's no kind of gag to put in an act. What I have in mind is something like this."

Blackjack Bracken told a joke. It was a childish one and in poor taste.

"I don't believe that is quite my style," I said.

"All right, what would you suggest?"

"I thought that I might lecture your patrons on the higher ethic."

"Look, George Albert, my patrons don't even have the lower ethic."

"And just what sort of recompense are we talking about?" I asked.

"Billy and I had about settled on a hundred and fifty a week."

"A hundred and fifty for whom?"

"Why, for Billy."

"I say a hundred and fifty for myself, and ten percent for Billy as my agent."

"Say, this blob's real smart, isn't he, Billy?"

"Too smart."

"Yes sir, George Albert, you're one smart blob. What kind of contract have you signed with Billy here?"

"No contract."

"Just a gentlemen's agreement?"

"No agreement."

"Billy, you can't hold him in a cage without a contract. That's slavery. It's against the law."

"But, Blackjack, a blob isn't people."

"Try proving that in court. Will you sign a contract with me, George Albert?"

"I will not dump Billy. He befriended me and gave me a home with the turtles and snakes. I will sign a joint contract with the two of you. We will discuss terms tomorrow—after I have estimated the attendance both here and at the night club."

III

Of the walking grubs (who call themselves "people") there are two kinds, and they place great emphasis on the difference. From this stems a large part of their difficulties. This distinction, which is one of polarity, cuts quite across the years and ability and station of life. It is not confined only to the people, but also involves apparently all the beings on the planet Florida.

It appears that a person is committed to one or the other polarity at the beginning of life, maintaining that polarity until death. The interlocking attraction-repulsion complex set up by these two opposable types has deep emotional involvements. It is the cause of considerable concern and disturbance, as well as desire and inspiration. There is a sort of poetic penumbra about the whole thing that tends to disguise its basic simplicity, expressible as a simultaneous polarity equation.

Complete segregation of the two types seems impossible. If it has ever been tried, it has now been abandoned as impractical.

There is indeed an intangible difference between the two types, so that before that first day at the Reptile Ranch was finished, I was able to differentiate between the two more than ninety percent of the time. The knowledge of this difference in polarity seems to be intuitive.

These two I will call the Beta and Gamma, or Boy and Girl types. I began to see that this opposability of the two types was one of the great driving forces of the people.

In the evening I was transported to the night club and I was a success. I would not entertain them with blue jokes or blue lyrics, but the patrons seemed fascinated by my simple imitations of all the instruments of the orchestra and my singing of comic ballads that Eustace had taught me in odd moments that day. They were also interested in the way that I drank gin, that is emptying the bottle without breaking the seal. (It seems that the grub-people are unable to absorb a liquid without making direct contact with it.)

And I met Margaret, one of the "girl" singers. I had been wondering to which type of people I might show affinity. Now I knew. I was definitely a Beta type, for I was attracted to Margaret, who was unmistakably a Gamma. I began to understand the queer effect that these types have on each other.

She came over to my cage.

"I want to rub your head for luck before I go on," she said.

"Thank you, Margaret," I replied, "but that is not my head."

She sang with incomparable sadness, with all the sorrow and sordidness that appear to be the lot of the unfortunate Gammas. It was the essence of melancholy made into music. It was a little bit like the ghost music of the asteroid Artemis, a little like the death chants on Dolmena. Sex and sorrow. Nostalgia. Regret.

Her singing shook me with a yearning that had no precedent.

She came back to my cage.

"You were wonderful, Margaret," I said.

"I'm always wonderful when I'm singing for my supper. I am less wonderful in the rare times when I am well fed. But are you happy, little buddy?"

"I had become almost so, till I heard you sing. Now I am overcome with a sorrow and longing. Margaret, I am fascinated with you."

"I go for you too, blob. You're my buddy. Isn't it funny that the only buddy I have in the world is a blob. But if you'd seen some of the guys I've been married to—boy! I wouldn't insult you by calling them blobs. Have to go now. See you tomorrow night if they keep us both on."

* * * *

Now there was a problem to face. It was necessary that I establish control over my environment, and at once. How else could I aspire to Margaret?

I knew that the heart of the entire place here was neither the bar nor the entertainment therein, nor the cuisine, nor the dancing. The heart of the enterprise was the casino. Here was the money that mattered; the rest was but garnish.

I had them bring me into the gambling rooms.

I had expected problems of complexity here where the patrons worked for their gain or loss. Instead there was an almost amazing simplicity. All the games were based on a system of first aspect numbers. Indeed everything on the Planet Florida seemed based on first aspect numbers.

Now it is an elemental fact that first aspect numbers do not carry within them their own prediction. Nor were the people even possessed of the prediction key that lies over the very threshold of the second aspect series.

These people were actually wagering sums—the symbols of prosperity—blindly, not knowing for sure whether they would win or lose. They were selecting numbers by hunch or at random with no assurance of profit. They were choosing a hole for a ball to fall into without knowing whether that was the right hole.

I do not believe that I was ever so amazed at anything in my life. But here was an opportunity to establish control over my environment.

I began to play the games. Usually I would watch a round first, to be sure that I understood just what was going on. Then I would play a few times... as many as it took to break the game.

I broke game after game. When he could no longer pay me, Blackjack closed the casino in exasperation.

Then we played poker, he and I and several others. This was even more simple. I suddenly realized that the grub-people could see only one side of the cards at a time.

I played and won.

I owned the casino now, and all of those people were now working for me. Billy Wilkins also played with us, and in short order I also owned the Reptile Ranch.

Before the evening was over, I owned a race-track, a beach hotel, and a theatre in a place named New York. I had, in sufficient extent for my purpose, established control over my environment...

* * * *

Later. Now started the golden days. I increased my control and did what I could for my friends.

I got a good doctor for my friend and roommate the python, and he was now receiving treatment for his indigestion. I got a jazzy sports car for my friend Eustace imported from somewhere called Italy. And I buried Margaret in mink, for she had a fix on the fur of that mysterious animal. She enjoyed draping it about her in the form of coats, capes, cloaks, mantles, and stoles, though the weather didn't really require it.

I had now won several banks, a railroad, an airline, and a casino in somewhere named Havana.

"You are somebody now," said Margaret. "You really ought to dress better. Or are you dressed? I never know. I don't know if part of that is clothes or if all of it is you. But at least I've learned which is your head. I think we should be married in May. It's so common to be married in June. Just imagine me being Mrs. George Albert Leroy Ellery McIntosh! You know, we have become quite an item. And do you know there are three biographies of you out, Burgeoning Blob; The Blob from Way Out; The Hidden Hand Behind the Blob, What Does It Portend? And the Governor has invited us to dine tomorrow. I do wish you would learn to eat. If you weren't so nice, you'd be creepy. I always say there's nothing wrong with marrying a man, or a blob, with money. It shows foresight on the part of a girl. You know you will have to get a blood test? You had better get it tomorrow. You do have blood, don't you?"

I did, but not, of course, of the color and viscosity of hers. But I could give it that color and viscosity temporarily. And it would react negative in all the tests.

She mused, "They are all jealous of me. They say they wouldn't marry a blob. They mean they couldn't. Do you have to carry that tin ball with you all the time?"

"Yes. It is my communication sphere. In it I record my thoughts. I would be lost without it."

"Oh, like a diary. How quaint."

Yes, those were the golden days. The grubs now appeared to me in a new light, for was not Margaret also a grub? Yet she seemed not so unfinished as the rest. Though lacking a natural outer covering, yet she had not the appearance of crawling out from under a rock. She was quite an attractive "girl." And she cared for me.

What more could I wish? I was affluent. I was respected. I was in control of my environment. And I could aid my friends of whom I had now acquired an astonishing number.

Moreover my old space-ineptitude sickness had left me. I never felt better in my life. Ah, golden days, one after the other like a pleasant dream. And soon I am to be married.

IV

There has been a sudden change. As on the Planet Hecube, where full summer turns into the dead of winter in minutes, to the destruction of many travelers, so was it here. My world is threatened!

It is tottering, all that I have built up. I will fight. I will fight. I will have the best lawyers on the planet. I am not done. But I am threatened…

Later. This may be the end. The appeal court has given its decision. A blob may not own property in Florida. A blob is not a person.

Of course I am not a person. I never pretended to be. But I am a personage. I will yet fight this thing…

Later. I have lost everything. The last appeal is gone. By definition I am an animal of indeterminate origin, and my property is being completely stripped from me.

I made an eloquent appeal—and it moved them greatly. There were tears in their eyes. But there was greed in the set of their mouths. They have a vested interest in stripping me. Each will seize a little.

And I am left a pauper, a vassal, an animal, a slave. This is always the last doom of the marooned, to be a despised alien at the mercy of a strange world.

Yet it should not be hopeless. I will have Margaret. Since my contract with Billy Wilkins and Blackjack Bracken, long since bought up, is no longer in effect, Margaret should be able to handle my affairs as a person. I believe that I have great earning powers yet, and I can win as much as I wish by gambling. We will treat this as only a technicality. We shall acquire new fortune. I will re-establish control over my environment. I will bring back the golden days. A few of my old friends are still loyal to me, Margaret, Pete the python, Eustace…

* * * *

Later. The world has caved in completely. Margaret has thrown me over.

"I'm sorry, blobby," she said, "but it just won't work. You're still nice, but without money you are only a blob. How would I marry a blob?"

"But we can earn more money. I am talented."

"No, you're box-office poison now. You were a fad, and fads die quickly."

"But Margaret, I can win as much as I wish by gambling."

"Not a chance, blobby. Nobody will gamble with you any more. You're through, blob. I will miss you, though. There will be a new blue note in my ballads when I sing for my supper, after the mink coats are all gone. Bye now."

"Margaret, do not leave me. What of all our golden days together?"

But all she said was "bye now."

And she was gone forever.

* * * *

I am desolate and my old space-ineptitude sickness has returned. My recovery was an illusion. I am so ill with awkwardness that I can no longer fly. I must crawl on the ground like one of the giant grubs. A curse on this planet Florida, and all its sister orbs! What a miserable world this is!

How could I have been taken in by a young Gamma type of the walking grub? Let her crawl back under her ancestral rocks with all the rest of her kind… No, no, I do not mean that. To me she will always remain a dream, a broken dream.

I am no longer welcome at the casino. They kicked me down the front steps.

I no longer have a home at the Reptile Ranch.

"Mr. George Albert," said Eustace, "I just can't afford to be seen with you any more. I have my position to consider, with a sport car and all that."

And Pete the python was curt.

"Well, big shot, I guess you aren't so big after all. And you were sure no friend of mine. When you had that doctor cure me of my indigestion, you left me with nothing but my bad conscience. I wish I could get my indigestion back."

"A curse on this world," I said.

"World, world, water, water, glug, glug," said the turtles in their tanks, my only friends.

So I have gone back into the woods to die. I have located my ejection mortar, and when I know that death is finally on me, I will fire off my communication sphere and hope it will reach the Galactic drift. Whoever finds it—friend, space traveler, you who were too impatient to remain on your own world—be you warned of this one! Here ingratitude is the rule and cruelty the main sport. The unfinished grubs have come out from under their rocks and they walk this world upside down with their heads in the air. Their friendship is fleeting, their promises are like the wind.

I am near my end.

THE SIX FINGERS OF TIME

He began by breaking things that morning. He broke the glass of water on his night stand. He knocked it crazily against the opposite wall and shattered it. Yet it shattered slowly. This would have surprised him if he had been fully awake, for he had only reached out sleepily for it.

Nor had he wakened regularly to his alarm; he had wakened to a weird, slow, low booming, yet the clock said six, time for the alarm. And the low boom, when it came again, seemed to come from the clock.

He reached out and touched it gently, but it floated off the stand at his touch and bounced around slowly on the floor. And when he picked it up again it had stopped, nor would shaking start it.

He checked the electric clock in the kitchen. This also said six o'clock, but the sweep hand did not move. In his living room the radio clock said six, but the second hand seemed stationary.

"But the lights in both rooms work," said Vincent. "How are the clocks stopped? Are they on a separate circuit?"

He went back to his bedroom and got his wristwatch. It also said six; and its sweep hand did not sweep.

"Now this could get silly. What is it that would stop both mechanical and electrical clocks?"

He went to the window and looked out at the clock on the Mutual Insurance Building. It said six o'clock, and the second hand did not move.

"Well, it is possible that the confusion is not limited to myself. I once heard the fanciful theory that a cold shower will clear the mind. For me it never has, but I will try it. I can always use cleanliness for an excuse."

The shower didn't work. Yes, it did: the water came now, but not like water; like very slow syrup that hung in the air. He reached up to touch it there hanging down and stretching. And it shattered like glass when he touched it and drifted in fantastic slow globs across the room. But it had the feel of water, wet and pleasantly cool. And in a quarter of a minute or so it was down over his shoulders and back, and he luxuriated in it. He let it soak his head and it cleared his wits at once.

"There is not a thing wrong with me. I am fine. It is not my fault that the water is slow this morning and other things awry."

He reached for the towel and it tore to pieces in his hands like porous wet paper.

Now he became very careful in the way he handled things. Slowly, tenderly, and deftly he took them so that they would not break. He shaved himself without mishap in spite of the slow water in the lavatory also.

Then he dressed himself with the greatest caution and cunning, breaking nothing except his shoe laces, a thing that is likely to happen at any time.

"If there is nothing the matter with me, then I will check and see if there is anything seriously wrong with the world. The dawn was fairly along when I looked out, as it should have been. Approximately twenty minutes have passed; it is a clear morning; the sun should now have hit the top several stories of the Insurance Building."

But it had not. It was a clear morning, but the dawn had not brightened at all in the twenty minutes. And that big clock still said six. It had not changed.

Yet it had changed, and he knew it with a queer feeling. He pictured it as it had been before. The hour and the minute hand had not moved noticeably. But the second hand had moved. It had moved a third of the dial.

So he pulled up a chair to the window and watched it. He realized that, though he could not see it move, yet it did make progress. He watched it for perhaps five minutes. It moved through a space of perhaps five seconds.

"Well, that is not my problem. It is that of the clock maker, either a terrestrial or a celestial one."

But he left his rooms without a good breakfast, and he left them very early. How did he know that it was early since there was something wrong with the time? Well, it was early at least according to the sun and according to the clocks, neither of which institutions seemed to be working properly.

He left without a good breakfast because the coffee would not make and the bacon would not fry. And in plain point of fact the fire would not heat. The gas flame came from the pilot light like a slowly spreading stream or an unfolding flower. Then it burned far too steadily. The skillet remained cold when placed over it; nor would water even heat. It had taken at least five minutes to get the water out of the faucet in the first place.

He ate a few pieces of leftover bread and some scraps of meat.

In the street there was no motion, no real motion. A truck, first seeming at rest, moved very slowly. There was no gear in which it could move so slowly. And there was a taxi which crept along, but Charles Vincent had to look at it carefully for some time to be sure that it was in motion. Then he received a shock. He realized by the early morning light that the driver of it was dead. Dead with his eyes wide open!

Slowly as it was going, and by whatever means it was moving, it should really be stopped. He walked over to it, opened the door, and pulled on the brake. Then he looked into the eyes of the dead man. Was he really dead?

It was hard to be sure. He felt warm. But, even as Vincent looked, the eyes of the dead man had begun to close. And close they did and open again in a matter of about twenty seconds.

This was weird. The slowly closing and opening eyes sent a chill through Vincent. And the dead man had begun to lean forward in his seat. Vincent put a hand in the middle of the man's chest to hold him upright, but he found the forward pressure as relentless as it was slow. He was unable to keep the dead man up.

So he let him go, watching curiously; and in a few seconds the driver's face was against the wheel. But it was almost as if it had no intention of stopping there. It pressed into the wheel with dogged force. He would surely break his face. Vincent took several holds on the dead man and counteracted the pressure somewhat. Yet the face was being damaged, and if things were normal, blood would have flowed.

The man had been dead so long however, that (though he was still warm) his blood must have congealed, for it was fully two minutes before it began to ooze.

"Whatever I have done, I have done enough damage," said Vincent. "And, in whatever nightmare I am in, I am likely to do further harm if I meddle more. I had better leave it alone."

He walked on down the morning street. Yet whatever vehicles he saw were moving with an incredible slowness, as though driven by some fantastic gear reduction. And there were people here and there frozen solid. It was a chilly morning, but it was not that cold. They were immobile in positions of motion, as though they were playing the children's game of Statues.

"How is it," said Charles Vincent, "that this young girl (who I believe works across the street from us) should have died standing up and in full stride? But, no. She is not dead. Or, if so, she died with a very alert expression. And—oh, my God, she's doing it too!"

For he realized that the eyes of the girl were closing, and in the space of no more than a quarter of a second they had completed their cycle and were open again. Also, and this was even stranger, she had moved, moved forward in full stride. He would have timed her if he could, but how could he when all the clocks were crazy? Yet she must have been taking about two steps a minute.

He went into the cafeteria. The early morning crowd that he had often watched through the windows was there. The girl who made flapjacks in the window had just flipped one and it hung in the air. Then it floated over as if caught by a slight breeze, and sank slowly down as if settling in water.

The breakfasters, like the people in the street, were all dead in this new way, moving with almost imperceptible motion. And all had apparently died in the act of drinking coffee, eating eggs, or munching toast. And if there were only time enough, there was even a chance that they would get the drinking, eating, and munching done with, for there was the shadow of movement in them all.

The cashier had the register drawer open and money in her hand, and the hand of the customer was outstretched for it. In time, somewhere in the new leisurely time, the hands would come together and the change be given. And so it happened. It may have been a minute and a half, or two minutes, or two and a half. It is always hard to judge time, and now it had become all but impossible.

"I am still hungry," said Charles Vincent, "but it would be foolhardy to wait for service here. Should I help myself? They will not mind if they are dead. And if they are not dead, in any case it seems that I am invisible to them."

He wolfed several rolls. He opened a bottle of milk and held it upside down over his glass while he ate another roll. Liquids had all become perversely slow.

But he felt better for his erratic breakfast. He would have paid for it, but how?

He left the cafeteria and walked about the town as it seemed still to be quite early, though one could depend on neither sun nor clock for the time any more. The traffic lights were unchanging. He sat for a long time in a little park and watched the town and the big clock in the Commerce Building tower; but like all the clocks it was either stopped or the hand would creep too slowly to be seen.

It must have been just about an hour till the traffic lights changed, but change they did at last. By picking a point on the building across the street and watching what moved past it, he found that the traffic did indeed move. In a minute or so, the entire length of a car would pass the given point.

He had, he recalled, been very far behind in his work and it had been worrying him. He decided to go to the office, early as it was or seemed to be.

He let himself in. Nobody else was there. He resolved not to look at the clock and to be very careful of the way he handled all objects because of his new propensity for breaking things. This considered, all seemed normal there. He had said the day before that he could hardly catch up on his work if he put in two days solid. He now resolved at least to work steadily until something happened, whatever it was.

For hour after hour he worked on his tabulations and reports. Nobody else had arrived. Could something be wrong? Certainly something was wrong. But this was not a holiday. That was not it.

Just how long can a stubborn and mystified man plug away at his task? It was hour after hour after hour. He did not become hungry nor particularly tired. And he did get through a lot of work.

"It must be half done. However it has happened, I have caught up on at least a day's work. I will keep on."

He must have continued silently for another eight or ten hours.

He was caught up completely on his back work.

"Well, to some extent I can work into the future. I can head up and carry over. I can put in everything but the figures of the field reports."

And he did so.

"It will be hard to bury me in work again. I could almost coast for a day. I don't even know what day it is, but I must have worked twenty hours straight through and nobody has arrived. Perhaps nobody ever will arrive. If they are moving with the speed of the people in the nightmare outside, it is no wonder they have not arrived."

He put his head down on his arms on the desk. The last thing he saw before he closed his eyes was the misshapen left thumb that he had always tried to conceal a little by the way he handled his hands.

"At least I know that I am still myself. I'd know myself anywhere by that."

Then he went to sleep at his desk.

Jenny came in with a quick click-click-click of high heels, and he wakened to the noise.

"What are you doing dozing at your desk, Mr. Vincent? Have you been here all night?"

"I don't know, Jenny. Honestly I don't."

"I was only teasing. Sometimes when I get here a little early I take a catnap myself."

The clock said six minutes till eight and the second hand was sweeping normally. Time had returned to the world. Or to him. But had all that early morning of his been a dream? Then it had been a very efficient dream. He had accomplished work that he could hardly have done in two days. And it was the same day that it was supposed to be.

He went to the water fountain. The water now behaved normally. He went to the window. The traffic was behaving as it should. Though sometimes slow and sometimes snarled, yet it was in the pace of the regular world.

The other workers arrived. They were not balls of fire, but neither was it necessary to observe them for several minutes to be sure they weren't dead.

"It did have its advantages," Charles Vincent said. "I would be afraid to live with it permanently, but it would be handy to go into for a few minutes a day and accomplish the business of hours. I may be a case for the doctor. But just how would I go about telling a doctor what was bothering me?"

Now it had surely been less than two hours from his first rising till the time that he wakened to the noise of Jenny from his second sleep. And how long that second sleep had been, or in which time enclave, he had no idea. But how account for it all? He had spent a long while in his own rooms, much longer than ordinary in his confusion. He had walked the city mile after mile in his puzzlement. And he had sat in the little park for hours and studied the situation. And he had worked at his own desk for an outlandish long time.

Well, he would go to the doctor. A man is obliged to refrain from making a fool of himself to the world at large, but to his own lawyer, his priest, or his doctor he will sometimes have to come as a fool. By their callings they are restrained from scoffing openly.

Dr. Mason was not particularly a friend. Charles Vincent realized with some unease that he did not have any particular friends, only acquaintances and associates. It was as though he were of a species slightly apart from his fellows. He wished now a little that he had a particular friend.

But Dr. Mason was an acquaintance of some years, had the reputation of being a good doctor, and besides Vincent had now arrived at his office and been shown in. He would either have to—well, that was as good a beginning as any.

"Doctor, I am in a predicament. I will either have to invent some symptoms to account for my visit here, or make an excuse and bolt, or tell you what is bothering me, even though you will think I am a new sort of idiot."

"Vincent, every day people invent symptoms to cover their visits here, and I know that they have lost their nerve about the real reason for coming. And every day people do make excuses and bolt. But experience tells me that I will get a larger fee if you tackle the third alternative. And, Vincent, there is no new sort of idiot."

Vincent said, "It may not sound so silly if I tell it quickly. I awoke this morning to some very puzzling incidents. It seemed that time itself had stopped, or that the whole world had gone into super-slow motion. The water would neither flow nor boil, and fire would not heat food. The clocks, which I first believed had stopped, crept along at perhaps a minute an hour. The people I met in the streets appeared dead, frozen in lifelike attitudes. And it was only by watching them for a very long time that I perceived that they did indeed have motion. One car I saw creeping slower than the most backward snail, and a dead man at the wheel of it. I went to it, opened the door, and put on the brake. I realized after a time that the man was not dead. But he bent forward and broke his face on the steering wheel. It must have taken a full minute for his head to travel no more than ten inches, yet I was unable to prevent his hitting the wheel. I then did other bizarre things in a world that had died on its feet. I walked many miles through the city, and then I sat for hours in the park. I went to the office and let myself in. I accomplished work that must have taken me twenty hours. I then took a nap at my desk. When I awoke on the arrival of the others, it was six minutes to eight in the morning of the same day, today. Not two hours had passed from my rising, and time was back to normal. But the things that happened in that time that could never be compressed into two hours."

"One question first, Vincent. Did you actually accomplish the work of many hours?"

"I did. It was done, and done in that time. It did not become undone on the return of time to normal."

"A second question. Had you been worried about your work, about being behind?"

"Yes. Emphatically."

"Then here is one explanation. You retired last night. But very shortly afterward you arose in a state of somnambulism. There are facets of sleep-walking which we do not at all understand. The time-out-of-focus interludes were parts of a walking dream of yours. You dressed and went to your office and worked all night. It is possible to do routine tasks in a somnambulistic state rapidly and even feverishly, with an intense concentration—to perform prodigies. You may have fallen into a normal sleep there when you had finished, or you may have been awakened directly from your somnambulistic trance on the arrival of your co-workers. There, that is a plausible and workable explanation. In the case of an apparently bizarre happening, it is always well to have a rational explanation to fall back on. They will usually satisfy a patient and put his mind at rest. But often they do not satisfy me."

"Your explanation very nearly satisfies me, Dr. Mason, and it does put my mind considerably at rest. I am sure that in a short while I will be able to accept it completely. But why does it not satisfy you?"

"One reason is a man I treated early this morning. He had his face smashed, and he had seen—or almost seen—a ghost: a ghost of incredible swiftness that was more sensed than seen. The ghost opened the door of his car while it was going at full speed, jerked on the brake, and caused him to crack his head. This man was dazed and had a slight concussion. I have convinced him that he did not see any ghost at all, that he must have dozed at the wheel and run into something. As I say, I am harder to convince than my patients. But it may have been coincidence."

"I hope so. But you also seem to have another reservation."

"After quite a few years in practice, I seldom see or hear anything new. Twice before I have been told a happening or a dream on the line of what you experienced."

"Did you convince your patients that it was only a dream?"

"I did. Both of them. That is, I convinced them the first few times it happened to them."

"Were they satisfied?"

"At first. Later, not entirely. But they both died within a year of their first coming to me."

"Nothing violent, I hope."

"Both had the gentlest deaths. That of senility extreme."

"Oh. Well, I'm too young for that."

"I would like you to come back in a month or so."

"I will, if the delusion or the dream returns. Or if I do not feel well."

After this Charles Vincent began to forget about the incident. He only recalled it with humor sometimes when again he was behind in his work.

"Well, if it gets bad enough I may do another sleepwalking act and catch up. But if there is another aspect of time and I could enter it at will, it might often be handy."

Charles Vincent never saw his face at all. It is very dark in some of those clubs and the Coq Bleu is like the inside of a tomb. He went to the clubs only about once a month, sometimes after a show when he did not want to go home to bed, sometimes when he was just plain restless.

Citizens of the more fortunate states may not know of the mysteries of the clubs. In Vincent's the only bars are beer bars, and only in the clubs can a person get a drink, and only members are admitted. It is true that even such a small club as the Coq Bleu had thirty thousand members, and at a dollar a year that is a nice sideline. The little numbered membership cards cost a penny each for the printing, and the member wrote in his own name. But he had to have a card—or a dollar for a card—to gain admittance.

But there could be no entertainments in the clubs. There was nothing there but the little bar room in the near darkness.

The man was there, and then he was not, and then he was there again. And always where he sat it was too dark to see his face.

"I wonder," he said to Vincent (or to the bar at large, though there were no other customers and the bartender was asleep), "I wonder if you have ever read Zurbarin on the Relationship of Extradigitalism to Genius?"

"I have never heard of the work nor of the man," said Vincent. "I doubt if either exists."

"I am Zurbarin," said the man.

Vincent hid his misshapen left thumb. Yet it could not have been noticed in that light, and he must have been crazy to believe there was any connection between it and the man's remark. It was not truly a double thumb. He was not an extradigital, nor was he a genius.

"I refuse to become interested in you," said Vincent. "I am on the verge of leaving. I dislike waking the bartender, but I did want another drink."

"Sooner done than said."

"What is?"

"Your glass is full."

"It is? So it is. Is it a trick?"

"Trick is the name for anything either too frivolous or too mystifying for us to comprehend. But on one long early morning of a month ago, you also could have done the trick, and nearly as well."

"Could I have? How would you know about my long early morning—assuming there to have been such?"

"I watched you for a while. Few others have the equipment to watch you with when you're in the aspect."

So they were silent for some time, and Vincent watched the clock and was ready to go.

"I wonder," said the man in the dark, "if you have read Schimmelpenninck on the Sexagintal and the Duodecimal in the Chaldee Mysteries?"

"I have not and I doubt if anyone else has. I would guess that you are also Schimmelpenninck and that you have just made up the name on the spur of the moment."

"I am Schimm, it is true, but I made up the name on the spur of a moment many years ago."

"I am a little bored with you," said Vincent, "but I would appreciate it if you'd do your glass-filling trick once more."

"I have just done so. And you are not bored; you are frightened."

"Of what?" asked Vincent, whose glass was in fact full again.

"Of reentering a dread that you are not sure was a dream. But there are advantages to being both invisible and inaudible."

"Can you be invisible?"

"Was I not when I went behind the bar just now and fixed you a drink?"

"How?"

"A man in full stride goes at the rate of about five miles an hour. Multiply that by sixty, which is the number of time. When I leave my stool and go behind the bar, I go and return at the rate of three hundred miles an hour. So I am invisible to you, particularly if I move while you blink."

"One thing does not match. You might have got around there and back, but you could not have poured."

"Shall I say that mastery over liquids is not given to beginners? But for us there are many ways to outwit the slowness of matter."

"I believe that you are a hoaxer. Do you know Dr. Mason?"

"I know that you went to see him. I know of his futile attempts to penetrate a certain mystery. But I have not talked to him of you."

"I still believe that you are a phony. Could you put me back into the state of my dream of a month ago?"

"It was not a dream. But I could put you again into that state."

"Prove it."

"Watch the clock. Do you believe that I can point my finger at it and stop it for you? It is already stopped for me."

"No, I don't believe it. Yes, I guess I have to, since I see that you have just done it. But it may be another trick. I don't know where the clock is plugged in."

"Neither do I. Come to the door. Look at every clock you can see. Are they not all stopped?"

"Yes. Maybe the power has gone off all over town."

"You know it has not. There are still lighted windows in those buildings, though it is quite late."

"Why are you playing with me? I am neither on the inside nor the outside. Either tell me the secret or say that you will not tell me."

"The secret isn't a simple one. It can only be arrived at after all philosophy and learning have been assimilated."

"One man cannot arrive at that in one lifetime."

"Not in an ordinary lifetime. But the secret of the secret (if I may put it that way) is that one must use part of it as a tool in learning. You could not learn all in one lifetime, but by being permitted the first step—to be able to read, say, sixty books in the time it took you to read one, to pause for a minute in thought and use up only one second, to get a day's work accomplished in eight minutes and so have time for other things—by such ways one may make a beginning. I will warn you, though. Even for the most intelligent, it is a race."

"A race? What race?"

"It is a race between success, which is life, and failure, which is death."

"Let's skip the melodrama. How do I get into the state and out of it?"

"Oh, that is simple, so easy that it seems like a gadget. Here are two diagrams I will draw. Note them carefully. This first, envision it in your mind and you are in the state. Now this second one, envision, and you are out of it."

"That easy?"

"That deceptively easy. The trick is to learn why it works—if you want to succeed, meaning to live."

So Charles Vincent left him and went home, walking the mile in a little less than fifteen normal seconds. But he still had not seen the face of the man.

There are advantages intellectual, monetary, and amorous in being able to enter the accelerated state at will. It is a fox game. One must be careful not to be caught at it, nor to break or harm that which is in the normal state.

Vincent could always find eight or ten minutes unobserved to accomplish the day's work. And a fifteen-minute coffee break could turn into a fifteen-hour romp around the town.

There was this boyish pleasure in becoming a ghost: to appear and stand motionless in front of an onrushing train and to cause the scream of the whistle, and to be in no danger, being able to move five or ten times as fast as the train; to enter and to sit suddenly in the middle of a select group and see them stare, and then disappear from the middle of them; to interfere in sports and games, entering a prize ring and tripping, hampering, or slugging the unliked fighter; to blue-shot down the hockey ice, skating at fifteen hundred miles an hour and scoring dozens of goals at either end while the people only know that something odd is happening.

There was pleasure in being able to shatter windows by chanting little songs, for the voice (when in the state) will be to the world at sixty times its regular pitch, though normal to oneself. And for this reason also he was inaudible to others.

There was fun in petty thieving and tricks. He would take a wallet from a man's pocket and be two blocks away when the victim turned at the feel. He would come back and stuff it into the man's mouth as he bleated to a policeman.

He would come into the home of a lady writing a letter, snatch up the paper and write three lines and vanish before the scream got out of her throat.

He would take food off forks, put baby turtles and live fish into bowls of soup between spoonfuls of the eater.

He would lash the hands of handshakers tightly together with stout cord. He unzipped persons of both sexes when they were at their most pompous. He changed cards from one player's hand to another's. He removed golf balls from tees during the backswing and left notes written large "YOU MISSED ME" pinned to the ground with the tee.

Or he shaved mustaches and heads. Returning repeatedly to one woman he disliked, he gradually clipped her bald and finally gilded her pate.

With tellers counting their money, he interfered outrageously and enriched himself. He snipped cigarettes in two with a scissors and blew out matches, so that one frustrated man broke down and cried at his inability to get a light.

He removed the weapons from the holsters of policemen and put cap pistols and water guns in their places. He unclipped the leashes of dogs and substituted little toy dogs rolling on wheels.

He put frogs in water glasses and left lighted firecrackers on bridge tables.

He reset wrist watches on wrists, and played pranks in men's rooms.

"I was always a boy at heart," said Charles Vincent.

Also during those first few days of the controlled new state, he established himself materially, acquiring wealth by devious ways, and opening bank accounts in various cities under various names, against a time of possible need.

Nor did he ever feel any shame for the tricks he played on unaccelerated humanity. For the people, when he was in the state, were as statues to him, hardly living, barely moving, unseeing, unhearing. And it is no shame to show disrespect to such comical statues.

And also, and again because he was a boy at heart, he had fun with the girls.

"I am one mass of black and blue marks," said Jenny one day. "My lips are sore and my front teeth feel loosened. I don't know what in the world is the matter with me."

Yet he had not meant to bruise or harm her. He was rather fond of her and he resolved to be much more careful. Yet it was fun, when he was in the state and invisible to her because of his speed, to kiss her here and there in out-of-the-way places. She made a nice statue and it was good sport. And there were others.

"You look older," said one of his co-workers one day. "Are you taking care of yourself? Are you worried?"

"I am not," said Vincent. "I never felt better or happier in my life."

But now there was time for so many things—time, in fact, for everything. There was no reason why he could not master anything in the world, when he could take off for fifteen minutes and gain fifteen hours. Vincent was a rapid but careful reader. He could now read from a hundred and twenty to two hundred books in an evening and night; and he slept in the accelerated state and could get a full night's sleep in eight minutes.

He first acquired a knowledge of languages. A quite extensive reading knowledge of a language can be acquired in three hundred hours world time, or three hundred minutes (five hours) accelerated time. And if one takes the tongues in order, from the most familiar to the most remote, there is no real difficulty. He acquired fifty for a starter, and could always add any other any evening that he found he had a need for it. And at the same time he began to assemble and consolidate knowledge. Of literature, properly speaking, there are no more than ten thousand books that are really worth reading and falling in love with. These were gone through with high pleasure, and two or three thousand of them were important enough to be reserved for future rereading.

History, however, is very uneven; and it is necessary to read texts and sources that for form are not worth reading. And the same with philosophy. Mathematics and science, pure or physical, could not, of course, be covered with the same speed. Yet, with time available, all could be mastered. There is no concept ever expressed by any human mind that cannot be comprehended by any other normal human mind, if time is available and it is taken in the proper order and context and with the proper preparatory work.

And often, and now more often, Vincent felt that he was touching the fingers of the secret; and always, when he came near it, it had a little bit the smell of the pit.

For he had pegged out all the main points of the history of man; or rather most of the tenable, or at least possible, theories of the history of man. It was hard to hold the main line of it, that double road of rationality and revelation that should lead always to a fuller and fuller development (not the fetish of progress, that toy word used only by toy people), to an unfolding and growth and perfectibility.

But the main line was often obscure and all but obliterated, and traced through fog and miasma. He had accepted the Fall of Man and the Redemption as the cardinal points of history. But he understood now that neither happened only once, that both were of constant occurrence; that there was a hand reaching up from that old pit with its shadow over man. And he had come to picture that hand in his dreams (for his dreams were especially vivid when in the state) as a six-digited monster reaching out. He began to realize that the thing he was caught in was dangerous and deadly.

Very dangerous.

Very deadly.

One of the weird books that he often returned to and which continually puzzled him was the Relationship of Extradigitalism to Genius, written by the man whose face he had never seen, in one of his manifestations.

It promised more than it delivered, and it intimated more than it said. Its theory was tedious and tenuous, bolstered with undigested mountains of doubtful data. It left him unconvinced that persons of genius (even if it could be agreed who or what they were) had often the oddity of extra fingers and toes, or the vestiges of them. And it puzzled him what possible difference it could make.

Yet there were hints here of a Corsican who commonly kept a hand hidden, or an earlier and more bizarre commander who wore always a mailed glove, of another man with a glove between the two; hints that the multiplex-adept, Leonardo himself, who sometimes drew the hands of men and often those of monsters with six fingers, may himself have had the touch. There was a comment of Caesar, not conclusive, to the same effect. It is known that Alexander had a minor peculiarity; it is not known what it was; this man made it seem that this was it. And it was averred of Gregory and Augustine, of Benedict and Albert and Acquinas. Yet a man with a deformity could not enter the priesthood; if they had it, it must have been in vestigial form.

There were cases for Charles Magnut and Mahmud, for Saladin the Horseman and for Akhnaton the King; for Homer (a Seleuciad-Greek statuette shows him with six fingers strumming an unidentified instrument while reciting); for Pythagoras, for Buonarroti, Santi, Theotokopolous, van Rijn, Robusti.

Zurbarin catalogued eight thousand names. He maintained that they were geniuses. And that they were extradigitals.

Charles Vincent grinned and looked down at his misshapen or double thumb.

"At least I am in good though monotonous company. But what in the name of triple time is he driving at?"

And it was not long afterward that Vincent was examining cuneiform tablets in the State Museum. These were a broken and not continuous series on the theory of numbers, tolerably legible to the now encyclopedic Charles Vincent. And the series read in part:

> "On the divergence of the basis itself and the confusion caused—for it is five, or it is six, or ten or twelve, or sixty or a hundred, or three hundred and sixty or the double hundred, the thousand. The reason, not clearly understood by the people, is that Six and the Dozen are first, and Sixty is a compromise in condescending to the people. For the five, the ten are late, and are no older than the people themselves. It is said, and credited, that people began to count by fives and tens from the number of fingers on their hands. But before the people the—by the reason that they had—counted by sixes and twelves. But Sixty is the number of time, divisible by both, for both must live together in time, though not on the same plane of time—"

Much of the rest was scattered. And it was while trying to set the hundreds of unordered clay tablets in proper sequence that Charles Vincent created the legend of the ghost in the museum.

For he spent his multi-hundred-hour nights there studying and classifying. Naturally he could not work without light, and naturally he could be seen when he sat still at his studies. But as the slow-moving guards attempted to close in on him, he would move to avoid them, and his speed made him invisible to them. They were a nuisance and had to be discouraged. He belabored them soundly and they became less eager to try to capture him.

His only fear was that they would some time try to shoot him to see if he were ghost or human. He could avoid a seen shot, which would come at no more than two and a half times his own greatest speed. But an unperceived shot could penetrate dangerously, even fatally, before he twisted away from it.

He had fathered legends of other ghosts, that of the Central Library, that of University Library, that of the John Charles Underwood Jr. Technical Library. This plurality of ghosts tended to cancel out each other and bring believers into ridicule. Even those who had seen him as a ghost did not admit that they believed in the ghosts.

He went back to Dr. Mason for his monthly checkup.

"You look terrible," said the Doctor. "Whatever it is, you have changed. If you can afford it, you should take a long rest."

"I have the means," said Charles Vincent, "and that is just what I will do. I'll take a rest for a year or two."

He had begun to begrudge the time that he must spend at the world's pace. From now on he was regarded as a recluse. He was silent and unsociable, for he found it a nuisance to come back to the common state to engage in conversation, and in his special state voices were too slow-pitched to intrude into his consciousness.

Except that of the man whose face he had never seen.

"You are making very tardy progress," said the man. Once more they were in a dark club. "Those who do not show more progress we cannot use. After all, you are only a vestigial. It is probable that you have very little of the ancient race in you. Fortunately those who do not show progress destroy themselves. You had not imagined that there were only two phases of time, had you?"

"Lately I have come to suspect that there are many more," said Charles Vincent.

"And you understand that only one step cannot succeed?"

"I understand that the life I have been living is in direct violation of all that we know of the laws of mass, momentum, and acceleration, as well as those of conservation of energy, the potential of the human person, the moral compensation, the golden mean, and the capacity of human organs. I know that I cannot multiply energy and experience sixty times without a compensating increase of food intake, and yet I do it. I know that I cannot live on eight minutes' sleep in twenty-four hours, but I do that also. I know that I cannot reasonably crowd four thousand years of experience into one lifetime, yet unreasonably I do not see what will prevent it. But you say I will destroy myself."

"Those who take only the first step destroy themselves."

"And how does one take the second step?"

"At the proper moment you will be given the choice."

"I have the most uncanny feeling that I will refuse the choice."

"From present indications, you will refuse it. You are fastidious."

"You have a smell about you, Old Man without a face. I know now what it is. It is the smell of the pit."

"Are you so slow to learn that?"

"It is the mud from the pit, the same from which the clay tablets were formed, from the old land between the rivers. I've dreamed of the six-fingered hand reaching up from the pit and overshadowing us all. And I have read: 'The people first counted by fives and tens from the number of fingers on their hands. But before the people—for the reason that they had—counted by sixes and twelves.' But time has left blanks in those tablets."

"Yes, time in one of its manifestations has deftly and with a purpose left those blanks."

"I cannot discover the name of the thing that goes in one of those blanks. Can you?"

"I am part of the name that goes into one of those blanks."

"And you are the man without a face. But why is it that you overshadow and control people? And to what purpose?"

"It will be long before you know those answers."

"When the choice comes to me, it will bear very careful weighing."

After that a chill descended on the life of Charles Vincent, for all that he still possessed his exceptional powers. And he seldom now indulged in pranks.

Except for Jennifer Parkey.

It was unusual that he should be drawn to her. He knew her only slightly in the common world and she was at least fifteen years his senior. But now she appealed to him for her youthful qualities, and all his pranks with her were gentle ones.

For one thing this spinster did not frighten, nor did she begin locking her doors, never having bothered about such things before. He would come behind her and stroke her hair, and she would speak out calmly with that sort of quickening in her voice: "Who are you? Why won't you let me see you? You are a friend, aren't you? Are you a man, or are you something else? If you can caress me, why can't you talk to me? Please let me see you. I promise that I won't hurt you."

It was as though she could not imagine that anything strange would hurt her. Or again when he hugged her or kissed her on the nape, she would call: "You must be a little boy, or very like a little boy, whoever you are. You are good not to break my things when you move about. Come here and let me hold you."

It is only very good people who have no fear at all of the unknown.

When Vincent met Jennifer in the regular world, as he more often now found occasion to do, she looked at him appraisingly, as though she guessed some sort of connection.

She said one day: "I know it is an impolite thing to say, but you do not look well at all. Have you been to a doctor?"

"Several times. But I think it is my doctor who should go to a doctor. He was always given to peculiar remarks, but now he is becoming a little unsettled."

"If I were your doctor, I believe I would also become a little unsettled. But you should find out what is wrong. You look terrible."

He did not look terrible. He had lost his hair, it is true, but many men lose their hair by thirty, though not perhaps as suddenly as he had. He thought of attributing it to the air resistance. After all, when he was in the state he did stride at some three hundred miles an hour. And enough of that is likely to blow the hair right off your head. And might that not also be the reason for his worsened complexion and the tireder look that appeared in his eyes? But he knew that this was nonsense. He felt no more air pressure when in his accelerated state than when in the normal one.

He had received his summons. He chose not to answer it. He did not want to be presented with the choice; he had no wish to be one with those of the pit. But he had no intention of giving up the great advantage which he now held over nature.

"I will have it both ways," he said. "I am already a contradiction and an impossibility. The proverb was only the early statement of the law of moral compensation: 'You can't take more out of a basket than it holds.' But for a long time I have been in violation of the laws and balances. 'There is no road without a turning,' 'Those who dance will have to pay the fiddler,' 'Everything that goes up comes down,' But are proverbs really universal laws? Certainly. A sound proverb has the force of universal law; it is but another statement of it. But I have contradicted the universal laws. It remains to be seen whether I have contradicted them with impunity. 'Every action has its reaction.' If I refuse to deal with them, I will provoke a strong reaction. The man without a face said that it was always a race between full knowing and destruction. Very well, I will race them for it."

They began to persecute him then. He knew that they were in a state as accelerated from his as his was from the normal. To them he was the almost motionless statue, hardly to be told from a dead man. To him they were by their speed both invisible and inaudible. They hurt him and haunted him. But still he would not answer the summons.

When the meeting took place, it was they who had to come to him, and they materialized there in his room, men without faces.

"The choice," said one. "You force us to be so clumsy as to have to voice it."

"I will have no part of you. You all smell of the pit, of that old mud of the cuneiforms of the land between the rivers, of the people who were before the people."

"It has endured a long time, and we consider it as enduring forever. But the Garden which was in the neighborhood—do you know how long the Garden lasted?"

"I don't know."

"That all happened in a single day, and before nightfall they were outside. You want to throw in with something more permanent, don't you."

"No. I don't believe I do."

"What have you to lose?"

"Only my hope of eternity."

"But you don't believe in that. No man has ever really believed in eternity."

"No man has ever either entirely believed or disbelieved in it," said Charles Vincent.

"At least it cannot be proved," said one of the faceless men. "Nothing is proved until it is over with. And in this case, if it is ever over with, then it is disproved. And all that time would one not be tempted to wonder, 'What if, after all, it ends in the next minute?'"

"I imagine that if we survive the flesh we will receive some sort of surety," said Vincent.

"But you are not sure either of such surviving or receiving. Now *we* have a very close approximation of eternity. When time is multiplied by itself, and that repeated again and again, does that not approximate eternity?"

"I don't believe it does. But I will not be of you. One of you has said that I am too fastidious. So now will you say that you'll destroy me?"

"No. We will only let you be destroyed. By yourself, you cannot win the race with destruction."

After that Charles Vincent somehow felt more mature. He knew he was not really meant to be a six-fingered thing of the pit. He knew that in some way he would have to pay for every minute and hour that he had gained. But what he had gained he would use to the fullest. And whatever could be accomplished by sheer acquisition of human knowledge, he would try to accomplish.

And he now startled Dr. Mason by the medical knowledge he had picked up, the while the doctor amused him by the concern he showed for Vincent. For he felt fine. He was perhaps not as active as he had been, but that was only because he had become dubious of aimless activity. He was still the ghost of the libraries and museums, but was puzzled that the published reports intimated that an old ghost had replaced a young one.

He now paid his mystic visits to Jennifer Parkey less often. For he was always dismayed to hear her exclaim to him in his ghostly form: "Your touch is so changed. You poor thing! Is there anything at all I can do to help you?"

He decided that somehow she was too immature to understand him, though he was still fond of her. He transferred his affections to Mrs. Milly Maltby, a widow at least thirty years his senior. Yet here it was a sort of girlishness in her that appealed to him. She was a woman of sharp wit and real affection, and she also accepted his visitations without fear, following a little initial panic.

They played games, writing games, for they communicated by writing. She would scribble a line, then hold the paper up in the air whence he would cause it to vanish into his sphere. He would return it in half a minute, or half a second by her time, with his retort. He had the advantage of her in time with greatly more opportunity to think up responses, but she had the advantage over him in natural wit and was hard to top.

They also played checkers, and he often had to retire apart and read a chapter of a book on the art between moves, and even so she often beat him; for native talent is likely to be a match for accumulated lore and codified procedure.

But to Milly also he was unfaithful in his fashion, being now interested (he no longer became enamored or entranced) in a Mrs. Roberts, a great-grandmother who was his elder by at least fifty years. He had read all the data extant on the attraction of the old for the young, but he still could not explain his successive attachments. He decided that these three examples were enough to establish a universal law: that a woman is simply not afraid of a ghost, though he touches her and is invisible, and writes her notes without hands. It is possible that amorous spirits have known this for a long time, but Charles Vincent had made the discovery himself independently.

When enough knowledge is accumulated on any subject, the pattern will sometimes emerge suddenly, like a form in a picture revealed where before it was not seen. And when enough knowledge is accumulated on all subjects, is there not a chance that a pattern governing all subjects will emerge?

Charles Vincent was caught up in one last enthusiasm. On a long vigil, as he consulted source after source and sorted them in his mind, it seemed that the pattern was coming out clearly and simply, for all its amazing complexity of detail.

"I know everything that they know in the pit, and I know a secret that they do not know. I have not lost the race—I have won it. I can defeat them at the point where they believe themselves invulnerable. If controlled hereafter, we need at least not be controlled by them. It is all falling together now. I have found the final truth, and it is they who have lost the race. I hold the key. I will now be able to enjoy the advantage without paying the ultimate price of defeat and destruction, or of collaboration with them.

"Now I have only to implement my knowledge, to publish the fact, and one shadow at least will be lifted from mankind. I will do it at once. Well, nearly at once. It is almost dawn in the normal world. I will sit here a very little while and rest. Then I will go out and begin to make contact with the proper persons for the disposition of this thing. But first I will sit here a little while and rest."

And he died quietly in his chair as he sat there.

Dr. Mason made an entry in his private journal: "Charles Vincent, a completely authenticated case of premature aging, one of the most clear-cut in all gerontology. This man was known to me for years, and I here aver that as of one year ago he was of normal appearance and physical state, and that his chronology is also correct, I having also known his father. I examined the subject during the period of his illness, and there is no question at all of his identity, which has also been established for the record by fingerprinting and other means. I aver that Charles Vincent at the age of thirty is dead of old age, having the appearance and organic condition of a man of ninety."

Then the doctor began to make another note: "As in two other cases of my own observation, the illness was accompanied by a certain delusion and series of dreams, so nearly identical in the three men as to be almost unbelievable. And for the record, and no doubt to the prejudice of my own reputation, I will set down the report of them here."

But when Dr. Mason had written that, he thought about it for a while.

"No, I will do no such thing," he said, and he struck out the last lines he had written. "It is best to let sleeping dragons lie."

And somewhere the faceless men with the smell of the pit on them smiled to themselves in quiet irony.

THE WAGONS

"But when did they have them first? Did they always have them? Who were the first ones to have them?"

"To have what?"

"The wagons. Did they always have wagons?"

"I guess they almost always had them. They had them a long time."

"Did the Indians have them?"

"No. Not at first. They didn't have the horse or wagon either at first. But they had the one almost as soon as the other."

"Did the Spanish have them?"

"Yes, they always had them. They used pack mules too. But they also used the wagon. Why do you ask?"

"Every night after the fire dies down I hear wagons going along the ridge. They sound like real old wagons and I can never find the tracks in the morning. Is that an old wagon road along the ridge?"

"Yes, I think that is an old wagon road. They often went along the ridge just below the sky line."

Jimmy was nine, and Jim was twenty years older. They both liked to camp out all summer. They traveled in a Ford pickup with an extra drum of gas in the back. They slept on the ground in their rolls and lived on coffee and bacon and flapjacks. They fished in the holes under the cottonwoods and shot jackrabbits and prairie dogs. The father and son were very close on these trips. And they went to ground in the short grass and brush country as though they had lived there for hundreds of years.

"Did they always go west—the wagons?"

"Why no, Jimmy, they couldn't always go west. They went in all directions."

"It seems to me they must have gone west most of the time."

Jimmy hacked out brush with a cradle and bolo. He gathered buffalo chips and cow chips. It was always his job to build the campfire.

"Was there ever a town at Cielito?"

"Yes, there was a little town there once I think, a tent town or a cabin town. I have heard that there was a little town there."

"I don't mean a little town. I mean a big town with square after square and wagons solid around them. Was there a big wagon town there a long time ago?"

"I don't know, Jimmy. I never heard of it."

"Was there a different kind of wagon that didn't have the same sort of tongue? It had a different creak, and the horses didn't sound the same way when they stomp."

"There were the ox wagons. They were hitched higher and rolled more. And on very early wagons the front wheels did not pivot and the tongue was pegged some way to the under carriage or axle itself. And a very long time ago the wagons were pulled by Onagers and Przewalski horses."

"That's the kind of horses. That's what I hear at night."

They had cuervo to eat. They rigged it on a spit to roast. It wasn't so bad if you called it cuervo. Lots of birds are all dark meat. All the wild birds are all dark meat. If you want chicken you can eat it at home.

"What did the Spanish call the wagons?"

"Carro."

"That's a cart, that isn't a wagon."

"Carro grande."

"That's a big cart. A big cart isn't a wagon. They're different."

"I don't know what they called them then, Jimmy."

"I think they probably had a long name with a squeak in the middle. Were the wagons always covered?"

"I guess they were covered for a long time."

"I think they had tents on wagons before they had them anywhere else. I think they had houses on wagons before they had them anywhere else. I guess those were the first houses."

"They had them a long time ago."

"Do you think Cielito had another name once?"

"I never heard of it if it had."

"I think that once it was called Hammadj or Plaustrumopolis."

"Where did you get names like that, Jimmy?"

"I just remembered them. I remember a lot of things like that. I'm pretty sure the wagon town was called a name like those. Could we go to Cielito in the morning and camp there tomorrow night?"

"Yes, we'll go there if you want to. There would be water there."

"Yes, there would have to be water there if they had all those horses there at one time."

"All what horses?"

"Why, if they had about ten thousand wagons there every night, a lot of them would have four or six or even eight horses. That would be a lot of horses."

"That would be quite a few, Jimmy. There is an old windmill about a mile from here and you can hear it creak at night. That may be the sound you think is wagons."

"No, I know where that old windmill is. And I know where there's a second one that you don't know about. But that's not what I hear for the wagons. If I couldn't tell wagons from windmills I'd turn in my ears."

"You'd look funny without them, Jimmy."

"I look funny with them too. I don't believe you believe I hear the wagons at all."

"Yes, I think you hear them, Jimmy."

After supper Jimmy told his father a story about prairie dogs.

"You think you know all about them but I bet you don't even know this. You see, in the very middle of every prairie dog town and about four feet down there is a pile of gold. The reason that the prairie dogs have little pouches in the sides of their cheeks is so they can carry the nuggets. All the prairie dog burrows in a town are connected and they all go back to the gold pile. Now this is the way it is run. When an owl comes to eat a prairie dog, the prairie dog has to give him one gold nugget to keep from being eaten. That's the only way they can do it, for the owl can go down the holes too and see in the dark. When the rattlesnake comes to eat a prairie dog, the prairie dog has to give him two nuggets. That's the only way it can work. If they ever run out of gold, then pretty soon they will run out of prairie dogs. Sometimes you will see an old prairie dog town that is deserted. What happened is that they ran out of gold and were all eaten."

"What do the owls and rattlesnakes do with the gold?"

"Different things. Sometimes the owls give it to the crows to keep them from pestering them in the daytime. Sometimes the rattlesnakes give it to the bull snakes to leave them alone. The rattlesnakes are afraid of the bull snakes."

"Well who gets the gold finally?"

"Old sharpies, snake hunters and crow hunters, and coyote hunters. The coyotes get gold from both the snakes and the crows for not killing them. There are coyote hunters that people wonder how they make a living they kill so few coyotes and the bounty is so low. They don't kill hardly any coyotes, but they sure do get a lot of gold."

"Where did you get a story like that?"

"I got it from a primitive. You remember the little Mexican at the store in Aguila that I talked to while you were buying supplies? He told me that story. He was pretty primitive. You said that when you get stories from the primitives themselves they are most likely to be authentic."

"Yes, I think your story is authentic."

Jimmy got out his guitar. He couldn't play very well but he liked to try. He played and sang *Cattle Call*, *Rye Whisky*, *Wagon Wheels*, *Camp Town Race Track*, *Chisholm Trail*, *Wagon Wheels*, *Frankie and Johnny*, *Red Wing*, *Way Out West in Kansas*, *Wagon Wheels*, *Streets of Laredo*, *Trail of the Lonesome Pine, Golden Slippers, Wagon Wheels, Blue Tail Fly, Hot Time in the Old Town, Way Back in the Hills, Wagon Wheels, Blues in the Night, Wabash Cannon Ball, Wreck of the Old Ninety-Seven, Wagon Wheels, Empty Saddles, In a Little Spanish Town, The Old Grey Goose is Dead, Sweet Geneveve, Wagon Wheels, Ramona, Tree in the Meadow, Mule Train, Wild Goose Song, Wagon Wheels.* He sang about an hour and a half. Then he did *Wagon Wheels* once more, and afterwards rolled up in his blanket and went to sleep.

Now here was the problem he considered as he slept. His father had said the wagons couldn't go west all the time. How could they go west all the time? And yet whenever he heard them at night they were going west. He had heard hundreds of them night after night, all going west.

The only way they could all be going west was to keep going on around the world but this wasn't likely.

"There are a lot of things I don't understand about the wagon trains, but I understand more than anyone else because I'm the only one who even knows about them."

In the morning they loaded up and went to Cielito. There was only one house at Cielito. But one house is enough for a town to have if it is able to handle the business. It may be that towns of more than one house are unnecessary. There is certainly some excess when they have ten or a hundred or a thousand or even a million houses; that is too big for a town to be.

There was both a gas pump and a watering trough there, so no matter how one traveled he could have his fill. There were two very great windmills and a whole series of tanks. And there were chutes and pens and corrals. The one house was built like a spider for there were many wings and extensions to it. There was a smoke house and a bake house, a horse stable and a goat pen, a bunk room or hotel, a store, a dining room, a bar, a herreria or repair shop; likely there was something else in the other wings as they would hardly build them and then leave them empty.

The reason that Jimmy had wanted to come to Cielito is that there were three wagons there, one still in use, and two very old ones that had been retired. He did not ordinarily like to camp near a town, not even one of modest size like Cielito; he had explained to his father that it was bad policy to camp within eight or ten miles of a town, and Jim the father had usually deferred to his superior wisdom in this. Mrs. Munyos told him about the wagons. The oldest one had been there before she was born, abandonado, left, unclaimed, derelict.

"Maybe they will come back some night and take it and continue their journey." Jimmy suggested to her.

"I doubt it, Chico. It was here they stopped to eat the last of their horses. Then they went ahead on foot. But after only one day's walk they lay down and died, los pobres. My abuelo found them the next spring and buried them with a cross even though they were heretics."

"Can I have the wagon then?"

"It isn't serviceable. Half of it is taken for firewood, and you would be able to go only a little ways with no horses and only three wheels on the thing. But it is yours if you want to say it is. It is no use, only to play in."

That afternoon she told him a lot more about the wagons, and about something else.

"I will tell you something that nobody knows except me. This is that a long time ago before people had wagons, los osos had them."

"Los osos? The bears?"

"That's right, the bears. This was a long time ago before the bears got stubborn as they are now, and won't even talk anymore except a few of them who have been raised by people. But the bears used to be the masters of everything. They had the only mills, so if the people wanted to have their corn ground they had to come to the bears to have it done, or else do it with hand stones. And the bears were the only ones who knew how to make baskets or bottles or tonels, or blankets. Did you ever watch a basket-man make a basket? He holds it as a bear would and works it towards himself. That is because the bears first taught the trade to the people. So the bears had a lot of business and the people had to come to them for everything. And they had big cities with paved streets and all kinds of riches."

"Then what happened?"

"I don't know. I think the bears must have become proud and have been punished. Now they have to live in the hills and have forgotten how to talk, or are too stubborn to do it. And they don't make blankets or baskets or anything any more, except for just one bunch of them in a town away back in the hills. There is only the one bear town left. And even the things they still make, they don't make them very well, hardly better than the people make them now."

"What did the bears have to pull their wagons with if they didn't have any horses then?" Jimmy wanted to know.

"No horses? Oh, well, a long time ago before there were any horses, there was another animal that looked exactly like the horse. So if you would see the two together you couldn't tell which one was the horse and which one was the other animal. This other animal is what the bears used to pull their wagons."

"Oh, I didn't know about that."

"And now you see, it is all changed. Now it is we the people who are very rich and powerful, and the bears who are poor. Little boy, I don't think you believe my story."

"Dama, I do. It is a legend. My father says that when we hear a legend we should try to arrive at the anthropomorphic truth behind it."

"That should take you all afternoon. And when you find it you tell me what it is."

But it didn't take him all afternoon, it only took him a little while to find what it was.

"Those bears who made tonels and drove wagons couldn't have been bears. They must also have been people. They were big people and they walked heavy where the Indians walked light. They had a lot of hair and beards and this made them look like bears, especially if they wore bear skins or buffalo robes. And if they say there's another animal that looked like a horse, well it was a horse all right, they just said it wasn't. I never believed that about there weren't any horses till the Spanish came here. The Indians used to hide their horses every time the Spanish came to town so they wouldn't get stolen, and it's a good thing they did. I can see it all now."

After he got it figured out he went to Mrs. Munyos and explained to her how it was.

"Ho, that's all you know," she told him. "Bigger and hairier then the Indians were they? Why I'd make thirteen of you myself, and talk about hair, my marido has so much hair on him it's like he crawled inside an old buffalo carcass."

"Ho, that's all you know," said Jimmy. "My father has more hair. When we're camping we just carry empty mattress covers and every night my father pulls enough hair out of his chest to stuff two of them full, and that's what we sleep on."

"That much hair? I can hardly believe it."

"Well it's true. What did you say was the name of that bear town?"

"Why Villaoso, of course. But you have to go way back in the hills to find it. You follow the canyon all the way back till it's so narrow that even the birds have to fly sideways. And when you get to the end of it there is Villaoso, the bear town."

"How did they get the wagons in if it's so narrow?"

"What wagons? Oh, the wagons. Well they built them hinged so they could flatten them out so that all four wheels were on behind the other. And when they were past the narrow part they straightened them out again. Do you think that is a mentina? Let us see if you can find the anthropomorphic truth behind that, little boy."

Jimmy went to seek out his father who was drinking wine in the bar.

"Papa, could we go tomorrow and look for the town of Villaoso?"

"We will go and look for it."

"It is back in the hills and up at the end of the canyon."

"I heard her tell you where it is."

They ate that night in the house that is the town of Cielito, and they slept in the old wagon bed. And the next day they went out to find Villaoso, the town of the bears. They followed the canyon all morning until it was so narrow that the birds had to fly sideways, and the Ford could hardly go between the walls.

"Were the wagons ever as narrow as the Ford?"

"They had to be almost if they went through here."

When it became so boulder strewn that they could drive no longer, they left the Ford and walked. And it was right about there that they saw the first of the bears. And after a thousand yards they came to Villaoso itself where the cliffs close in. There were upward of thirty neat caves in the cliffs, but only five or six bears lounging around. The rest no doubt were out working somewhere.

And there was still a way between the cliffs just wide enough for a wagon, and the trail went on down to the plains on the other side. Jim went up the face of the cliff quite a ways and then roped Jimmy up. They had a nice den that it would take a very agile bear to reach.

"One thing worries me," said Jimmy. "I don't see any remnants of basketry or pottery or even a corn mill. I thought the bears here would at least keep up some of the arts. They don't even seem to have blankets, not even poor ones. For these really are bears. I thought at first they would turn out to be just hairy men."

Jim took the rifle and went back to the car before it got dark. He brought the supplies back up the cliff to the cave. He cut wood and brought it up too.

"Do you want a bear steak?"

"Oh no, dad, don't kill any of these. These might not be ordinary bears at all."

"You mustn't let the old stories get a hold of you, Jimmy."

They built a fire on the ledge to keep away the bears and mountain lions and devils, just as the first family in that region had done eighteen thousand and twelve years before. The figures are Jimmy's and are arrived at logically. For it was a reliable book he had read, and it gave the figure at eighteen thousand years; and it had been published twelve years before.

After supper Jimmy serenaded the bears with his guitar, and they looked up at him in the dusk and sat around like big dogs. And after that a coyote serenaded them from a distant cliff top.

"There are three coyotes," said Jimmy. "I can tell them by their voices. There is one reddish one almost as red as a fox. And there is one big gray grizzled one. And there is one with his tail full of cockleburs."

"No. There's only one," said Jim.

"Why, there's four more now, and that makes seven. There's one with a sort of black cross on his muzzle, and there's one with a crippled foot. And there's a chicken killer that still has feathers on his face. And there's one real young one. That makes seven."

"No. There is only one."

"There's six more from the other cliff and that makes thirteen. One of them has a white front foot. And one of them ran into a skunk this morning and has to stay a little off from the others. And there's the old boss coyote, and there's the one that's going to take him out someday. And there's a young female who has a couple of them excited. And there's a mean one with a slashed ear that doesn't get along with the others. I can tell what they're all like by their voices and there's thirteen of them."

"No," said Jim. "There's only one."

"Why, there's at least nine more now that just sounded from farther back. That'd make twenty-two. I know there's more than one coyote."

"Yes, you are right. Now there are two of them."

After a while they went to sleep and let the coyotes have it.

After a long time Jimmy heard the creaking and woke his father.

"It's the wagons. You sure ought to be able to hear them now."

"Yes, I believe I hear a wagon."

"There's at least a dozen, and I guess there are a hundred right behind them. There's one with a loose rim and they ought to fix it tomorrow. And there's one with a bad seat spring and it hits bottom every time they go over a boulder. And there's one with a tongue squeak, and one has a split spoke, you can tell by the way it grinds in the hub. And one has loose boards in the bed. And one is loaded too heavy on one side or the load has shifted, it gives a kind of twisting squeak. And one of them has a front wheel that sure could use something. And one of them has a colt tied behind and he's getting tired of it all. And one of them has a sort of harness rasp. They ought to dress it with a little oil. There's a lot of them, you can tell that right off."

"No. I think there's only one. I believe all those disabilities belong to one wagon."

"There's one horse has thrown a shoe and he goes tender on that foot. And one wagon has a lantern or something hanging under it with a squeaky handle. And one has a lot of stuff lashed on. Ropes have a sound when they stretch and give."

"I know they have, Jimmy. But there is only one wagon."

And there was only one. It came over the boulders up the canyon with a big load lashed on and a lantern swinging underneath and a colt tied on behind.

"Hola!" one of the wagon men called up to them by the fire.

"Hola!" said Jim.

"Oje!" said Jimmy. And the wagon went through the narrow pass where there was only an inch on either side, and on down the other slope of the divide.

"There really was only one," said Jimmy. "And I thought there was about a hundred. But that's the same wagon I heard the other night. They haul something into a little camp. They didn't have the colt the last time I heard it, but one night they had a burro on behind. I sure do like to listen to wagons."

A bull-bat swooped down from one cliff and up above the other one. Then another bull-bat swooped in the opposite direction. And directly a third one went the same way as the first.

"I'll bet there's a hundred bull-bats flying around," said Jimmy. "There's one that has double jointed wings, and one that has two white bars on the top and bottom side too. And there's one that doesn't eat anything but midge flies, and one that doesn't eat anything but sexton beetles. And one of them has two claws bit off by a prairie dog. I'll bet there's a hundred of them."

"No," said Jim. "There is only one."

SATURDAY YOU DIE

Besides being born (that is an ordeal, no less an ordeal because you forget it) the worst thing to be gone through is to be a new boy in a small Southern town.

There are reasons for this. First, the boys are tougher in the South. They go barefoot in April. They play with green snakes. They keep scorpions in fruit jars. They clang cow bells, and they pop whips. In the second place, all the boys are bigger than you are. But in the North they had all been your size.

Howard Glass, Stanely Savage, Clifford Welch, and that other boy whose name had not been learned yet, they were all bigger than Henry. Howard and Stanely would both go to school next year. Not only that, but Clifford and that other boy had already been to school, and next year they would be in the second grade.

So all the boys in town were bigger than Henry. And, though he would have been the last to admit it, they were all tougher too.

"If you ever tell anybody what we tell you we'll throw you in the ditch at Carter Road and you won't be able to get out," Howard Glass said. "And nobody will find you until the weed-cutter comes along, and then all they'll find is your bones."

"I never tell anything," Henry said steadfastly. "In all my life I never tell anything."

The ditch at Carter Road was the deepest one in town and Henry didn't know whether he'd be able to climb out of it or not. In the entire North there was nothing remotely like that ditch at Carter Road.

"Or else we'll bury you in the cave," said Howard Glass. "We have another cave under the floor of the first and we bury people there."

They did have a cave in this new town. In the North they had only talked about caves but nobody had ever seen one.

Howard's name was Glass, probably because he wore glasses, the only one besides grown people who ever did so. He had eyes as big as a cow's. Clifford Welsh said that if Howard had his glasses off then his eyes wouldn't be any bigger than anyone else's, but there was no way to prove this. Howard always had his glasses on and they made him look like an owl. But they didn't have owls here in the South. If they had, they were a different kind, and you wouldn't know them for what they were.

And there is this about the South; it is larger than it is in the North. This is because more than half the trees had been cut down or had never been there; the grass was heavy green; and there was no snow left on the north side of the houses, and perhaps there had never been. The water came from crank-handle cisterns instead of pump-handle pumps; and more of the town people kept cows. The squirrels were grey instead of red. The trees were different. And they had new kinds of birds, like scissortails, that nobody had ever seen before. It was less cloudy, and the days were longer. You could see a great deal farther as both the earth and the sky were everywhere of more extent. Other people have noticed other differences between the North and the South, but it was Henry who discovered the essential difference: it is larger in the South.

"After you bury them in the cave, how long before you let them out?" Henry asked.

"How would we let them out? After you're dead there's nothing to let out."

"Then you get to stay there all the time?"

"Sure. All the time. Except that the next Saturday we take you out again and cut you up." Howard's eyes were flecked green behind his glasses and were bigger than a cow's. "Then we cut the flesh off you and put it in jars to sell for crawfish bait. And we put your bones in a box and bury them again."

"But the first time you're buried, it's only for a week?"

"Yes, a week."

"That isn't so bad to be buried for a week if you know that you're going to get out again."

* * * *

The hill at the edge of town was named Doolen's Mountain. It was closer to Henry's house than to any of the others. There had been nothing like Doolen's Mountain in the North, and those people wouldn't have believed it if it were told to them. The cave was in the near flank of Doolen's Mountain, and Henry knew that he could get into the cave when the rest of the boys had gone home for dinner. They said it was their cave and he couldn't go in, but now he lived in the house closest to it.

But he didn't go into the cave on that first day: instead he climbed the mountain itself. It was three times as tall as a house, and it seemed to go down in five sides from the flat top of it.

Two of the fluted sides faced back into town. And down beyond the center one of the opposite sides there ran a long ragged ditch that twisted as far as the horizon through ragged pasture land. The other two country sides were green, but two different shades of green. One of them was blue-green and stretched to the limit of vision: it was winter wheat. One was bright green: a prairie-hay meadow coming to life.

There came some kind of bees or yellowjackets and chased Henry off the top of Doolen's Mountain. But he waited until he thought they would be gone, and then got a stick and went back up. He stayed there a long time. He threw rocks down the sides of the mountain. Then he happened to think: "If everybody would do that, then they'd use up the whole mountain and it'd be flat as the rest of the places and I'd have no place to climb." He threw no more rocks down. Instead he went down and got rocks, some of them the same ones he'd thrown down and others that couldn't be identified, and carried them back to the top to repair the damage.

Clifford Welch came up to the top of the mountain and sat down two feet away from Henry. They seemed not to notice each other, and for a long while each went about his own business. But it was Clifford who spoke first which pleased Henry, for he knew that in this he was the victor.

"If any of the other boys hurt you, you tell me," Clifford said. "I'm the biggest and I'll make them stop. When I tell anybody to do something they have to do it because they're all afraid of me."

"What if they hurt me next week when you're in school?"

"After school you tell me about it and I'll make them quit."

"What if they kill me?"

"Then I'll kill them."

That seemed satisfactory, but oddly it wasn't. Often there are things left over that worry you when they should be settled.

"Howard Glass says he's going to kill me and bury me in the cave," Henry said.

"Howard was just bragging. Last time was the first time we even let him watch. Stanely and I are the only ones who ever kill boys and bury them in the cave."

"Howard says it will be next Saturday."

"Yes. Next Saturday. We always do it on a Saturday."

"Are you really going to do it to me?"

"Unless there's another new boy moves to town before then. If another new boy moves here, we kill him instead of you. We always kill the last one to come."

"Maybe another new one will come," Henry said. They left it at that. It wasn't completely satisfactory, but it would have to do. So much had happened since last Saturday, with almost all of two days on the train, and most of one night in the depot in Kansas City, and other things besides that. Last Saturday was a long ways away, and the next one would be a long time coming.

"If a new boy comes to town, can I help you kill him?" Henry asked.

"We'll see," said Clifford. "Maybe we won't let you help with the first one, but there'll be others."

From the top of Doolen's Mountain, three times as high as a house, higher than some barns, you could see everything. There was no limit to your vision except the sky itself.

"I've been in five states," Henry said, "this one, and the one we left, and the two we came through on the way down here. And one week we went to South Dakota from Iowa when I was little. I've been in five states."

"What are states?" Clifford asked. And the bitter disappointment cut Henry like a butcher knife.

* * * *

But it was Stanely Savage who really told Henry what things were about. This was the next Monday when Clifford Welch and the other boy were in school. The other boy was named Quenton Quint. And on that day also, Howard Glass (the other one who didn't go to school yet) had to stay in his house on account of his abominable conduct:—which is no part of this history, and yet in a way it is, for Howard often behaved abominably, as Henry was to learn as the days went by. But this Monday there were only Henry and Stanely.

"Under our cave is another cave," Stanely said, "and it goes for miles. It comes out on a river or ocean, and the boats tie up there. We go there at night and trade with the pirate boats when they come up."

"But the cave is in Doolen's Mountain," Henry said, "and the only river that comes near Doolen's Mountain is the bayou, and it's only a ditch. How could the cave come out on a big river or ocean where boats tie up?"

But as soon as Henry had asked that, he knew that his objection was a flimsy one. In a story, a boy finds a door in a tree and goes in, and there are hundreds of houses and towns and a whole country that is different from the outside one. A lot of things are bigger on the inside than on the outside.

Naturally Stanely didn't answer Henry's objection, but he continued:

"All the pirates come here, Black Wolf and Dread Wolf and Captain Kidd and John Silver, and that other pirate who has one red eye and one black eye. He's the king of them all."

"What's his name?" Henry asked.

"We can't tell anybody his name. He's supposed to be hanged and drowned and not running loose. The pirates bring us live monkeys and parrots and gunny sacks full of gold. They bring us pearls as big as pigeon's eggs, and slaves in chains, and long swords, and those other kind of curved swords. They bring us guns with the barrel-ends like funnels, and red pants, and green pirates' coats."

"Where do you keep all that stuff? I never see any of it."

"We keep it hidden. We put part of it in the cave under our first cave. We keep part of it in other places. I keep my slave-in-chains in a little room up in the attic of my house that nobody knows is there but me. At night he comes down to my room and makes gold money for me. He grinds it out with a little grinder."

"What does he grind it out of?"

"He puts in old bolts and nuts and horseshoes and old milk-can covers."

"And it comes out gold money?"

"Sure it does. I got a whole roomful of it."

"Could I get a slave to make me some too?"

"No. You're too little. And besides, you'll be dead."

"What do you trade to the pirates for all that?"

"Hickory nuts and pecans mostly. They can't get them at sea. And bird's eggs. But the thing that is worth more than anything else is eyes. That's what we kill all the boys for, to get their eyes to trade to the pirates."

"What do they do with all the eyes?"

"Well, they nail them up on the top of the mast, or on one of those sticks that go out from the side of the mast. They tell those eyes to keep a sharp watch and give a signal if they see land or a ship or a whale."

"Is that what will happen to my eyes?"

"Yes. They'll nail them up on the highest part of the ship for a lookout."

"But if there's nothing left but my eyes, how will I give the signal when I see something? I won't have anything left to holler with."

"I think they give you a little bell to ring," Stanely said.

* * * *

There was more to it than that, of course. When they kill you they do different things to different parts of you. They sell some of you to Mr. Hockmeyer to put in his sausage. You know how he jokes about grinding boys up in his machine? He isn't joking. He really does it. He doesn't use much of them in each batch though: only one boy to half a dozen hogs. People like the taste of the sausage but they wouldn't buy it if they knew what was in it. And some of the bones can be used. The shooter of Clifford Welch has a fork made from a boy's wishbone. But the eyes are the most valuable part.

* * * *

It wasn't until Wednesday that Henry went into the cave itself. There wasn't much there: pieces of an old structo set, a hammer head without a handle, some hickory-nut shells, ashes from a fire, a jar full of poison water. Henry knew about the water: that is the way they killed you; they made you drink it and you fell down and died. It looked like other water, but it had scorpion poison in it.

The doorway to the lower cave, however, was ingeniously hidden. There are three ways to open a secret door. One is to find the edge of it and pry it up. One is to say the words that will make it open. One is to have someone show you how.

But Henry couldn't find any edge to it however far he dug. He tried different words, but they were not the right ones. So somebody would have to show him how. At least he'd get to go down to the lower cave Saturday when they killed him.

The rest of the week was filled with great expectation. Henry dreamed it out in the mornings as he sat in the cave, and in the afternoons as he sat on top of Doolen's Mountain. The appeal of a completely untrammeled existence has always been strong. It would be perfect to be no more than a pair of eyes. To be on the highest stick of a ship and to be able to see further than anybody else in the world, that would be a new sort of ultimate. From the very top you would be able to see whole islands that nobody else had seen, to see whole ships before they came into view. Being so high, you could see the tops and the backs of the clouds, and look at the inside of the cloud rooms. You could look down and see the green whales, bigger than catfish, snoozing in the weeds. And some day you would be able to see what made the first wave. The first wave pushes the next one, and that one pushes the one you see. But nobody has ever seen the first wave that starts them all.

And if you are nothing but two eyes, you can turn one of them to look at the other one. Or, with the two of them not tied together, you can be in two different places at one time, which nobody else can do. You can roll like marbles and go wherever you want to. You can hide in places and see people who can't see you. It is to be invisible. Moreover, you get to travel all over the world and work for the king of the pirates who has one red eye and one black eye. It is a unique existence, and very few boys have ever experienced it.

And so it was all through the week and into Friday dusk that Henry thought, into howling locust time, cricket time, June bug time (in the South they have June bugs in April), street-light time, star-light time. Then, in the twilight, there was a big truck in town, square as a cracker box, big as a train, and with red lights on the back and front of it. Cursing and straining men were moving crates half as big as a room, and boxes and trunks. They had opened up the old Shane house that had always been dark and locked and drawn-blinded and weed-choked. This evening it was full of light.

A little later, Mrs. Glass told Henry to come into her house and have some cake. What matter that Howard Glass acted abominably to him and twisted his arm! It was worth it for the cake. Henry went home happy afterwards, for the next day was Saturday and he would get to be killed and turned into a pair of eyes and ride on the highest part of a pirate ship and ring a bell when he saw a whale or land or a boat. He would be the lookout for the pirate king with one red eye and one black eye. He would get to see the world.

"You can give all my clothes away," he told his mother as he came home that evening. "After tomorrow, I won't be using them anymore." But she didn't know what he meant. Often she didn't.

* * * *

If you know what is going to happen, the last night in the old life can be an exciting one. The vision of the new and enlarged life will set you to dreaming without sleeping, and morning never comes soon enough.

The sun comes up earlier in the South, and Henry was around very early that Saturday morning, banging on doors. But he could get nobody up, nobody but the new boy. All the front porch of the Shane house was still piled up with crates and chairs in spite of all that had already been taken inside.

"Where do you come from?" Henry asked the new boy.

"Kansas."

"That isn't very far. We came through Kansas on our way down here. We came from three times that far away. What's your name?"

"Baxter."

"I've got a better name than that. My name is Henry. We have a cave but you can't go in it until you've been here longer. We have a mountain but you can't climb it yet. And if I told you what was going to happen to me today you wouldn't believe it. I get to go away where nobody else ever went before. You're only a new boy and things like that can't happen to you."

"A new boy!"

The world crashed to pieces. It clattered like tin cans on cement when it collapsed. For Baxter was a newer boy than Henry, and he would get to be killed instead of Henry. The greatest of all disasters had come as simply and quietly as that.

Baxter was a new boy moved to town. Baxter would get killed instead of Henry. And now Henry's chances were gone forever.

* * * *

Henry howled and turned and ran away. Baxter's mother came out.

"What did you do to that little boy to make him cry?" she asked.

"I didn't do anything to him. I don't know why he started to cry."

"You must have done something to make him cry. You have to be good and try to get along with the other boys. We're in a new town now."

* * * *

Henry ran in black horror—(Baxter instead of him)—out to the edge of town—(it would be Baxter's eyes and not his eyes)—past the cave with the other cave under it—(Baxter would get to see the Islands and Whales, Henry wouldn't get to see anything)—sobbing up to the top of Doolen's Mountain. He flung himself down and wept bitterly over his lost hopes.

TRY TO REMEMBER

1.

It isn't that professors are absent-minded. That is a canard, a joke thought up by somebody who should have been better employed. The fact is that sometimes professors have great presence of mind; they have to have. The fact is that professors are (or should be) very busy and thoughtful men, and that they are forced in the interests of time and efficiency to relegate the unessentials to the background.

Professor—what was that blamed name again?—well anyway, he had done so, he had swept all the unessentials quite out of the way. He carried a small black book prepared by his wife (it must have been his wife) in which all the unessential details of his regime were written down for his guidance and to save him time. On the cover were the words "Try to Remember," and inside was information copious and handy.

He picked it up now, from the table in front of him, and opened it.

"You are professor J. F. E. Diller," he read. "The J is for John. There is no use in burdening your mind with the meaning of the other two initials. You are known to your students as Killer Diller for no good reason beyond euphony, and you are called by me "Moxie" for my own reasons.

"You teach Middle Mayan Archeology. Please don't try to teach anything else. You don't know anything else. Your schedule is as follows:— But before you examine it, always look at your watch. It shows both the day of the week and the time of the day. It is on your left wrist. The best way I can tell you which is your left wrist is to say that it is the one that your watch is on."

And there followed the schedule with times and classes and building and room number, and indications as to whether the class was elementary or middle or advanced, and which text was used, Boch, or Mendoza y Carriba, or Strohspalter. And below the class schedule were other varied notes.

"You like every kind of meat except liver. Don't order it. You think you like it but you don't. You are always fearfully disappointed when you try to eat it. Eat anything else; you fortunately do not have to watch your calories. You drink Cuba Libres. Never take more than four drinks at one session, they make you so nutty. There is a little drink-counter in your left-hand pants pocket that I made for you. Flip it every time that you have a drink.

When you have had four, it will not flip again; so come on home. The best way I can tell you which is your left-hand pants pocket is that it is the one your drink-counter is in."

There was much more. The professor looked at his watch, looked at his schedule, saw that he still had a little time before his final class, glanced at the final entry in the book, "I love you, Emily," smiled, closed the small notebook, and put it in his pocket.

"Women have a satirical turn of mind," he said to his companion.

"What? Are you sure?" the companion asked. "Blenheim denies it, and the evidence in Creager is doubtful. And Pfirschbaum in his monumental monogram 'Satire und Geschlecht' has gone into the problem rather more thoroughly than most, and he is not of your opinion. And we have here on our own campus a fellow, Kearney, who is widely read in the field. If you have independent new evidence, you might go to him with it. He will appreciate it."

"No. I am sorry. I phrased myself badly. I should have said that my own wife, in a particular instance that has just come to my hand, shows flashes of satire. I realize the dangers of generalizing. As to making a statement about the mind of women generally, that is beyond my scope."

His next class by the schedule, and the final one of the day, was an elementary one in Middle Mayan Archeology, and the text, of course, was that of Boch. But the professor seldom stayed with the text long. He would ask the place of a student, read a paragraph or two out loud, and then begin to talk. Talking was one of the things he did best. He had humor and verve, and the students always liked him. And, if a man knows his subject (Did he know his subject? What an odd question! How could he be a professor if he didn't know his subject?), if a man knows his subject thoroughly, then he can afford to handle it lightly, and to toy, to elucidate, to digress.

So the hour went easily and pleasantly. Yet an odd thought began to crawl like a bug up his back, and it unsettled him. "I have been talking total nonsense," said the thought. "Now why would I be talking nonsense when I am competent and know my subject?"

And the thought slept, but did not die, when after class was over he went to the Scatterbrain Lounge to drink.

"Cuba Libre," he ordered confidently.

"Are you sure?" asked the girl.

It was only a split second to flip open the small pocket notebook. He had done it many times and was adept at it.

"That is correct," he said. "A Cuba Libre."

But a moment later there was another fly caught in the ointment where it beat futile wings and expired. In an indefinite manner things were not right.

"I have lost my drink-counter," said the professor, "and I never lose things, only misplace them. It is not in my left pocket, if that is the left one. And if the other one is the left pocket, why it is not in that one either? How will I know when I've had four drinks?"

"That's easy enough," said the girl. "I'll tell you."

"So are all unusual problems solved," said the professor, "by unusual means and flashes of intuition."

After the girl had told him that the drink he had just finished was his fourth, the professor, feeling woozy, had her call a taxi for him; then, looking in his notebook for his home address, he gave it to the driver and rode off feeling rosy and fine.

Then, after he had paid the driver, and with a quick glance at "I love you, Emily" on the last page of the notebook he went up to the house, went in, and kissed the beautiful Emily as hard as he knew how to. Then he put his hands on her shoulders and looked at her lovingly, and she at him.

"This is quite the best thing that has happened to me in a wonderful day," he said. "I had almost forgotten that you were so beautiful."

"It had nearly slipped my mind also," said Emily. "And it is very sweet to be reminded of it."

She was beautiful. And she had a look at once very affectionate and very, very quizzical; a woman full of humor and satire indeed.

"Pfirschbaum is wrong!" said the professor positively, "cataclysmically wrong. Could he but see that look on your face, so kind, so amused, so arch; he would realize just how wrong he is."

"I'm sure that he would. I would rather like to see the look on my face myself. It must be a study of mixed emotions. Oh, you're doing it again, you little wolf! How sweet you are! I wonder who invented kissing in the first place?"

"It is generally attributed to the Milesians, Emily, but there has lately appeared evidence that it may be even earlier. Emily, you are wonderful, wonderful."

"I know it. But keep telling me."

2.

Catherine came in then. She also had a quizzical look on her face, but there was something in it that was pretty dour too. And following her, and looking quite sheepish, was that little professor, what was his name? Oh yes, Diller.

The professor gave Emily one more kiss, and then turned to greet them. And suddenly a strange disquietude caught him in a grip of ice. "If he is Professor Diller, then who in multicolor blazes am I?"

Professors aren't really absent-minded. It is just that they learn to relegate details to the background. But sometimes they don't stay in the background, and now this detail was much to the fore. But the professor could think like a flash when necessary, and in no time at all he remembered not only who he was, but just what kind of trouble he was in.

But it didn't help matters when, as he was leaving with Catherine, Emily called after him "It was fun, Tommy. Let's do it again sometime."

Nor was Catherine inclined to be quiet when he sat at home next door with her and read in his own notebook (which he now had back from Professor Dillard, after that awful mix-up when the identical-appearing reminder books of the two men had apparently been lying together on the table in the teachers' lounge, and each man had mistakenly picked up the other's),—when he read in his own notebook:

> "You are professor T. K. C. Cromwell. The T is for Thomas. You teach Provencal and Early French Literature and teach it badly, but we must eat. This is your schedule. Never deviate from it or you will be lost—"

* * * *

Now, if he had had his own notebook all the time, he would never have made such series of silly mistakes. Most of the trouble that comes to people in this world comes from reading the wrong books.

"To think," said Catherine, "that a grown man could make a mistake like that, if it was a mistake. There is a point beyond which absent-mindedness is no longer a joke. How did you get by with your classes?"

"I don't know. I suspected once that I was talking total nonsense."

"And that little Killer Diller is as bad as you are. I was never so surprised in my life as when he waltzed in here and slapped me on... why I don't know how you men can get so confused."

"But we've explained how the notebooks must have got mixed up."

"I understand how the notebooks were mixed. I do not understand how you are so mixed. Emily is vastly amused over this. I am not so amused."

It isn't that professors are absent-minded. Anybody should have had sense enough not to have made the notebooks that much alike.

MCGONIGAL'S WORM

When it happened, it happened unnoticed. Though it affected all chordata on Earth (with a possible exception to be noted in a moment) nobody knew of it, not even the Prince of all chordata, Man himself. How could he have known of it so soon?

Though his lifeline had suddenly been cut, it was a long lifeline and death would still be far off. So it was not suspected for nearly twenty-four hours, not accepted even as a working theory for nearly three days, and not realized in its full implications for a week.

Now, what had occurred was a sudden and worldwide adynatogenesis of all chordata, not however, adynatotokos; this distinction for many years offered students of the phenomenon some hope.

And another hope was in the fact that one small but genuine member of chordate was not affected: an enteropneustron, a balanoglossida of the oddest sort, a creature known as McGonigal's Worm. Yet what hope this creature could offer was necessarily a small one.

The catastrophe was first sensed by a hobbyist about a day after it occurred. It was just that certain experiments did not act right and the proper results were not forthcoming. And on the second day (Monday) there were probably a hundred notations of quite unusual and unstatistical behavior, but as yet the pattern was not at all suspected.

On the third day a cranky and suspicious laboratory worker went to a supply house with the angry charge that he had been sold sterile mice. This was something that could not be ignored, and it is what brought the pattern of the whole thing into the open, with corroboration developing with explosive rapidity. Not completely in the open, of course, for fear of panic if it reached the public. Out throughout the learned community the news went like a seismic shock.

When it did reach the public a week later, though, it was greeted with hoots of laughter. The people did not believe it.

* * * *

"The cataloguing of evidence becomes tiresome," said Director Conrad of the newly originated Palingenesia Institute. "The facts are incontrovertible. There has been a loss of the power to conceive in sea squirt, lancelet, hag fish, skate, sea cat, fish, frog, alligator, snake, turtle, seal, porpoise, mouse, bat, bird, hog, horse, monkey, and man. It happened suddenly, perhaps instantaneously. We cannot find the cure. Yet it is almost certain that those children already in the womb will be the last born on Earth. We do not know whether it is from a natural cause or an enemy has done this to us. We have for ten months, tested nearly everything in the world and we have found no answer. Yet, oddly enough, there is no panic."

"Except among ourselves," said Appleby, his assistant, "whose province is its study. But the people have accepted it so completely that their main interest now is in the world sweepstakes, with the total sums wagered now in the billions."

"Yes, the betting on the last child to be born in the world. It will prove one point, at least. The old legal limit on posthumous paternity was a year and a day. Will it be surpassed? The Algerian claimant on all evidence has nearly three months to go. And the betters on the Afghan have not yet given up. The Spanish Pretender is being delayed, according to rumor, medically, and there are some pretty angry protests about this. It is not at all fair; we know that. But then a comprehensive set of rules was never drawn up to cover all nations; Spain simply chose not to join the pact. But there may be trouble if the Spanish backers try to collect."

"And there is also a newly heard of Mexican claimant."

"I give little credit to this Juanita-Come-Lately. If she was to be a serious contestant why was she not known of before?"

The Algerian claimant, however, was the winner. And the time was an unbelievable three hundred and eighty-eight days. So the last child on Earth, in all likelihood, had been born.

There were now about thirty institutes working on the problem, most of them on an international basis. Thirteen years had gone by and one hope had died. This was that those already in the womb at the time of catastrophe might themselves prove to be fertile. It was now seen that this would not prove so, unless for some reason it was to be quite a delayed fertility.

The Cosmic Causes Council had by no means come to a dead end. It had come to so many live ends as to be even more bewildering.

"The point," said Hegnar, in one of his yearly summaries, "is not whether sterility could have been caused by cosmic forces. Of course it could have been. It could have been caused in twenty ways. The miracle is that fertility had ever been possible. There must have been a shield built in for every danger. We know but scantily what some of them are. We do not know which has failed or why."

"And could the failure have been caused by an enemy?" asked an interlocutor.

"It could have been, certainly. Almost by definition we must call an enemy anything that can harm us. But that it was a conscious enemy is something else again. Who can say what cosmic forces are conscious? Or even what it means to be conscious?"

* * * *

However, the Possibility Searcher Institute had some spotted success. It had worked out a test, a valid test, of determining whether an individual yet remaining had the spark of possible fertility. And in only a few million tests it had found one male shrew, one male gannet, no less than three males of the yellow perch, one female alligator, and one female mud puppy, all of whom still possessed the potential. This was encouraging, but it did not solve the problem. No issue could be obtained from any possible pairing of these; not that it wasn't tried.

And when the possibility test was run on all the humans of the Earth, then it was that incredible and unsuspected success crowned the efforts of the institute. For, of a bare three billion persons tested, there were two who tested positive; and (good fortune beyond all hoping), one was male and the other was female.

So then the problem was solved. A few years had been lost, it is true, and several generations would be required to get the thing on a sound footing again. But life had been saved. Civilization could yet be transmitted. All was not lost.

Musha ibn Scmuel was an Arabian black, an unthrifty man of tenuous income. His occupation on the cardex was given as thief, but this may have been a euphemism. He was middle-aged and full of vigor, a plain man innocent of shoes or subtlety. He was guilty neither of the wine hatred of the Musselman nor the garrulousness of the Greek. He possessed his soul in quietude and Port Said whiskey and seldom stole more than he needed. And he had a special competence shared by no man in the world.

Cecilia Clutt was an attractive and snooty spinster of thirty five. She was a person of inherited as well as acquired wealth, and was an astute business woman and amateur of the arts. She did have a streak of stubbornness in her, but seldom revealed it unless she was crossed.

So, the first time she said no, it was hardly noticed. And the second time she said it, it was felt that she didn't quite understand the situation. So it was Carmody Overlark, the silky diplomat, who came to reason with her.

"You are the sole hope of the human race," he said to her. "In a way, you are the new Eve."

"I have heard the first one spoken badly of," said Cecilia.

"Yet her only fault was that she could be talked into something. I cannot."

"But this is important."

"Not really. If it is our time to disappear, then let us disappear with dignity. What you suggest is without it. It would leave us a little less than human."

"Miss Clutt, this is a world problem. You are only an individual."

"I am not *only* an individual. There is no such thing as only an individual. If ever a person can be spoken of as only an individual, then humanity has already failed."

"We have tried reason. Now by special emergency legislation, we are empowered to employ compulsion."

"We will see. I always did enjoy a good fight."

Those who read the State Histories of the period will know that it did not come off. But the reasons given there are garbled. "Unforeseen circumstances" cover a multitude of failures. But what really happened was this.

Musha ibn S. had been tractable enough. Though refusing to fly, he had come on shipboard readily. And it was not till they were out of the Inland Sea and on the Atlantic that he showed a certain unease. Finally he asked, reasonably enough, to be shown a picture of his bride. But his reaction on seeing it was not reasonable.

He screamed like a dying camel. And he jumped overboard. He was a determined swimmer and he was heading for home. A boat was put out and it gained on him. But, as it came up to him, he sounded. How deep he dived is not known, but he was never seen again.

On hearing of this, Cecilia Clutt was a little uncertain for the first time in her life. Just to be sure, she asked for a copy of the picture.

"Oh, that one," said Cecilia. "It is quite a nice picture, really. It flatters me a little. But what an odd reaction. What a truly odd reaction."

* * * *

There were repercussions on the economy. The primary schools were now all closed, except for a few turned over to retarded children. In a year or two the high schools would close also. The colleges would perhaps always be maintained, for adult education, and for their expanding graduate schools. Yet the zest for the future had diminished, even though the personal future of nobody had been abridged. New construction had almost ceased and multi-bedroom homes became a drag on the market. In a very few years there would be no additions at all to the workforce. Soon there would be no more young soldiers for the armies. And soon the last eyes ever would see the world with the poetic clearness that often comes with adolescence.

There had been a definite letdown in morals. Morals have declined in every generation since the first one, which itself left something to be desired. But this new generation was different. It was a tree that could not bear fruit, a hard-barked, selfish tree. Yet what good to look at it and shudder for the future? The future had already been disposed of.

Now there was a new hobby, a mania that swept the world, the Last Man Clubs, millions of them. Who would be the last person alive on Earth?

But still the institutes labored. The Capsule Institute in particular labored for the codification and preservation of all knowledge. For whom? For those who might come after. Who? Of what species? But still they worked at it.

And the oddest of the institutes was the Bare Chance Transmission Society. In spite of all derision and mockery, it persevered in its peculiar aim: to find some viable creature that could be educated or adapted or mutated to absorb human knowledge and carry on once more the human tradition.

What creature? What possible strain could it be from? What creature on Earth was unaffected?

Well, the largest of them was the giant squid. But it was not promising. It had shown no development in many millions of years; it did not seem capable of development or education. And, moreover, there are difficulties of rapport with a creature that only can live in the deep sea.

There were the insects. Bees and ants were capable of organization, though intelligence has been denied them. Spiders showed certain rugged abilities, and fruit flies. Special committees were appointed to study each. And then there were the fleas. Old flea-circus grifters were brought out of retirement and given positions of responsibility and power. If fleas could really be taught, then these men could teach them. But though fleas can be taught to wear microscopic spectacles they cannot be taught to read. It all seemed pretty futile.

And there were the crayfish, the snails, the starfish, the sea cucumber. There were the fresh water flat worm and the liver fluke. There were the polyp, the sponge, the cephalopod. But, after all, none of them was of the main line. They were of the ancestry that had failed. And what of the noble genealogy that had succeeded, that which had risen above all and had given civilization, the chordata? Of that noble line, was there nothing left? What was the highest form still producing?

McGonigal's Worm.

It was discouraging.

But for the careful study of M. W., as it was now known, a great new institute was now created. And to the M. W. Institute was channeled all the talent that seemed expedient.

And one of the first to go to work for the institute in a common capacity was a young lady of thirty-odd named Georgina Hickle. Young lady? Yes. Georgina was within months of being the youngest woman in the world.

She was a scatter-brained wife and disliked worms. But one must work and there were at that time no other jobs open.

But she was not impressed by the indoctrination given in this new laboratory.

"You must change your whole way of thinking," said the doctor who briefed them. "We are seeking new departures. We are looking for any possible breakthrough. You must learn to think of M. W. as the hope of the world."

"Oog," said Georgina.

"You must think of M. W. as your very kindred, as your cousin."

"Oog," said Georgina.

"You must think of him as your little brother that you have to teach, as your very child, as your cherished son."

"Oog, oog," said Georgina, for she disliked worms.

Nor was she happy on the job. She was not good at teaching worms. She believed them both stupid and stubborn. They did not have her sympathy, and after a few weeks they seemed to make her sick.

* * * *

But her ailment was a mysterious one. None of the young doctors had ever seen anything like it. And it was contagious. Other women in the bright new laboratory began to show similar symptoms. Yet contagion there was impossible, such extreme precautions had been taken for the protection of the worms.

But Georgina did not respond to treatment. And Hinkle's Disease was definitely spreading. Sharper young doctors fresh from the greatest medical schools were calling in. They knew all that was to be known about all the new diseases. But they did not know this.

Georgina felt queer now and odd things began to happen to her. Like that very morning on her way to work, that old lady had stared at her.

"Glory be," said the old lady, "a miracle." And she crossed herself.

And Georgina heard other comments.

"I don't believe it. It isn't possible," a man said.

"Well, it sure does look like it," said a woman.

So Georgina took off at noon to visit a psychiatrist and tell him that she imagined that people were staring at her and talking about her, and what should she do. It made her uneasy, she said.

"That's not what is making you uneasy," said the psychiatrist. Then he went with her to the laboratory to have a look at some of the other women suffering from this Hickle's Disease that he had been hearing about. After that, he called the young doctors at the laboratory aside for a consultation.

"I don't know by what authority you mean to instruct us," said one. "You haven't been upgraded in thirty years."

"I know it."

"You are completely out of touch with the latest techniques."

"I know it."

"You have been described—accurately, I believe—as an old fogy."

"I know that too."

"Then what could you tell us about a new appearance like Hickle's Disease?"

"Only that it is not really new. And not, properly speaking, a disease."

* * * *

That is why, even today, there are superstitious persons who keep Mc-Gonigal's Worms in small mesh cages in the belief that they insure fertility. It is rank nonsense and rose only because it was in the M. W. laboratory that the return of pregnancy was first noticed and was named for one of the women working there. It is a belief which dates back to that ancient generation, which very nearly became the last generation.

The official explanation is that the Earth and its solar system, for a period of thirty-five years, was in an area of mysterious cosmic radiation. And afterwards it drifted out of that area.

But there are many who still believe in the influence of the McGonigal's Worm.

THE POLITE PEOPLE OF PUDIBUNDIA

"Well, you will soon see for yourself, Marlow. Yes, I know there are peculiar stories about the place. There are about all places. The young pilots who have been there tell some amusing tales about it."

"Yes. They say the people there are very polite."

"That is the honorable ancestor of all understatements. One of the pilots, Conrad, told us that the inhabitants must always carry seven types of sunglasses with them. None of the Puds, you see, may ever gaze directly on another. That would be the height of impoliteness. They wear amber goggles when they go about their world at large, and these they wear when they meet a stranger. But, once they are introduced to him, then they must thereafter look on him through blue glasses. But at a blood relative they gaze through red, and at an in-law through yellow. There are equally interesting colours for other situations."

"I would like to talk to Conrad. Not that I doubt his reports. It is the things he did not report that interest me."

"I thought you knew he had died. Thrombosis, though he was sound enough when first certified."

"But if they are really people, then it should be possible to understand them."

"But they are not really people. They are metamorphics. They become people only out of politeness."

"Detail that a little."

"Oh, they're biped and of a size of us. They have a chameleon-like skin that can take on any texture they please, and they possess extreme plasticity of features."

"You mean they can take on the appearance of people at will?"

"So Bently reported."

"I hadn't heard of him."

"Another of the young pilots. According to Bently, not only do the Puds take on a human appearance, they take on the appearance of the human they encounter. Out of politeness, of course."

"Quite a tribute, though it seems extreme. Could I talk to Bently?"

"Also dead. A promising young man. But he reported some of the most amusing aspects of all: the circumlocutions that the Puds use in speaking our language. Not only is the Second Person eschewed out of politeness, but in a way all the other Persons also. One of them could not call you by your name, Marlow. He would have to say: 'One hears of one who hears of one of the noble name of Marlow. One hears of one even now in his presence.'

"Yes, that is quite a polite way of saying it. But it would seem that with all their circumlocutions they would be inefficient."

"Yet they are quite efficient. They do things so well that it is almost imperative that we learn from them. Yet for all our contacts, for all their extreme politeness coupled with their seeming openness, we have been able to learn almost nothing. We cannot learn the secret of the amazing productivity of their fields. According to Sharper, another of the young pilots, they suggest (though so circumspectly that it seems hardly a suggestion, certainly not a criticism) that if we were more polite to our own plants, the plants would be more productive for us; and if we gave the plants the ultimate of politeness, they would give us the ultimate of production."

"Could I talk to Sharper, or is he also—"

"No, he is not dead. He was quite well until the last several days. Now, however, he is ailing, but I believe it will be possible for you to talk to him before you leave, if he does not worsen."

"It would still seem difficult for the Puds to get anything done. Wouldn't a superior be too polite to give a reprimand to an inferior?"

"Probably. But Masters, who visited them, had a theory about it, which is that the inferior would be so polite and deferential that he would do his best to anticipate a wish or a desire, or would go to any lengths to learn the import of an unvoiced preference."

"Is Masters one of the young pilots?"

"No, an old-timer."

"Now you do interest me."

"Dead quite a few years. But it is you who interest me, Marlow. I have been told to give you all the information that you need about the Polite People of Pudibundia. And on the subject of the Polite People, I must also be polite. But—saving your presence, and one hears of one who hears and all that—what in gehenna is a captain in homicide on the Solar Police Force going to Pudibundia about?"

"About murder. That is all I ever go anywhere about. We once had a private motto that we would go to the end of the Earth to solve a case."

"And now you have amended your motto to 'to the end of the Earth and beyond'?"

"We have."

"But what have the Polite People to do with murder? Crime is unknown on Pudibundia."

"We believe, saving their feelings, that it may not be unknown there. And what I am going to find out is this. There have been pilots for many years who have brought back stories of the Puds, and there are still a few— a very few—young pilots alive to tell those stories. What I am going to find out is why there are no old pilots around telling those stories."

* * * *

It wasn't much of a trip for a tripper, six weeks. And Marlow was well received. His host also assumed the name of Marlow out of politeness. It would have been impossible to render his own name in human speech, and it would have been impossible for him to conceive of using any name except that of his guest, with its modifiers. Yet there was no confusion. Marlow was Marlow, and his host was the One-Million-Times-Lesser-Marlow.

"We could progress much faster," said Marlow, "if we dispense with these formalities."

"Or assumed them as already spoken," said the One-Million-Times-Lesser-Marlow. "For this, in private, and only in the strictest privacy, we use the deferential ball. Within it are all the formulae written minutely. You have but to pass the ball from hand to hand every time you speak, and it is as if the amenities were spoken. I will give you this for the time of your stay. I beg you never to forget to pass it from hand to hand every time you speak. Should you forget, I would not, of course, be allowed to notice it. But when you were gone, I should be forced to kill myself for the shame of it. For private reasons I wish to avoid this and therefore beseech you to be careful."

The One-Million-Times-Lesser-Marlow (hereafter to be called OM-TLM for convenience but not out of any lack of politeness) gave Marlow a deferential ball, about the size of a ping-pong ball. And so they talked.

"As a police official, I am particularly interested in the crime situation on Pud," said Marlow. "An index of zero is—well, if I could find a politer word I would use it—suspicious. And as you are, as well as I can determine, the head police official here, though in politeness your office would have another name, I am hoping that you can give me information."

"Saving your grace, and formula of a formula, what would you have me tell you about?"

"Suppose that a burglar (for politeness sake called something else) were apprehended by a policeman (likewise), what would happen?"

"Why, the policeman (not so called, and yet we must be frank) would rattle his glottis in the prescribed manner."

"Rattle his gl— I see. He would clear his throat with the appropriate sound. And then the burglar (not so called)?"

"Would be covered with shame, it is true, but not fatally. For the peace of his own soul, he would leave the site in as dignified a manner as possible."

"With or without boodle?"

"Naturally without. One apprehended in the act is obliged to abandon his loot. That is only common politeness."

"I see. And if the burglar (not so called) remains unapprehended? How is the loss of the goods or property recorded?"

"It goes into the coefficient of general diminution of merchandise, which is to say shrinkage, wastage or loss. At certain times or places this coefficient becomes alarmingly large. Then it is necessary to use extraordinary care; and in extreme cases a thrice removed burglar may become so ashamed of himself that he will die."

"That he will die of shame? Or is that a euphemism?"

"Let us say that it is a euphemism of a euphemism."

"Thrice-removed, I imagine. And what of other crimes?"

* * * *

Here OMTLM rattled his glottis in a nervous manner, and Marlow hurriedly transferred his deferential ball to the other hand, having nearly forgotten it.

"There being no crime, we can hardly speak of other crimes," said OMTLM. "But perhaps, in another manner of speaking, you refer to—"

"Crimes of violence," said Marlow.

"Saving your presence, and formula of a formula, what would we have to be violent about? What possible cause?"

"The usual: greed, lust, jealousy, anger, revenge, plain perversity."

"Here also it is possible for one to die of shame, sometimes the offender, sometimes the victim, sometimes both. A jealous person might permit both his wife and her paramour to die of shame. And the State in turn might permit him to perish likewise, unless there were circumstances to modify the degree of shame; then he might still continue to live, often in circumscribed circumstances, for a set number of years. Each case must be decided on its own merits."

"I understand your meaning. But why build a fence around it?"

"I do not know what you mean?"

"I believe that you do. Why are the Polite People of Pudibundia so polite? Is it simply custom?"

"It is more than that," said the polite Pud.

"Then there is a real reason for it? Can you tell it to me?"

"There is a real reason for it. I cannot tell it to you now, though, and perhaps not ever. But there is a chance that you may be given a demonstration of it just before you leave. And if you are very wise, you may be able then to guess the reason. I believe that there are several who have guessed it. I hope that we will have time for other discussions before you leave our sphere. And I certainly do hope that your stay on Pudibundia is a pleasant one. And now, saving your presence, we must part. Formula of a formula."

"Formula of a formula and all that," said Marlow, and went to discover the pleasures of Pudibundia.

Among the pleasures of Pud was Mitzi (Miniature-Image-a-Thousand-times-removed of the Zestful Irma) who had now shaped up into something very nice. And shaped up is the correct term.

At first Marlow was shocked by the appearance of all the females he met on Pud. Crude-featured, almost horse-faced, how could they all look like that? And he was even more shocked when he realized the reason. He had become used to the men there looking like himself out of politeness. And this—this abomination—was the female version of his own appearance!

But he was a man of resources. He took from his pocket a small picture of Irma that he always carried, and showed it to the most friendly of the girls.

"Could you possibly—"

"Look like that? Why, of course. Let me study it for a moment. Now, then."

So the girl assumed the face of Irma.

"Incredible," said Marlow, "except Irma is red-headed."

"You have only to ask. The photo is not colored and so I did not know. We will try this shade to start with."

"Close, but could you turn it just a little darker?"

"Of course."

And there she was Irma of the most interesting face and wonderful hair. But the picture had been of the face only. Below that the girl was a sack. If only there was some way to convey what was lacking. "You still are not pleased with me," said the Miniature-Image-a-Thousand-times-removed of the Zestful Irma (Mitzi). "But you have only to demonstrate. Show me with your hands."

Marlow, with his hands, sculptured in the air the figure of Irma as he remembered it, and Mitzi assumed the form, first face on, then face away, then in profile. And when they had it roughly, they perfected it, a little more here, a little less there. But there were points where his memory failed him.

"If you could only give me an idea of the convolutions of her ears," said Mitzi, "and the underlying structure of the metatarsus. My only desire is to please. Or shall I improvise where you do not remember?"

"Yes, do that, Mitzi."

138 | R.A. LAFFERTY

And how that girl could improvise!

* * * *

Marlow and Mitzi were now buddies. They made a large evening of it. They tied one on; formula of a formula, but they tied one on. They went on a thrice-removed bender. At the Betelgeuse Bar and Grill they partook of the cousin of the cousin of the alcohol itself in the form of the nono-rhumbeziod, made of nine kinds of rum. At the B-Flat Starlight Club, they listened to the newest and most exciting music on all Pudibundia. At Alligator John's, one checks his inhibitions at the door. Here one also checks his deferential ball.

Of course the formulae are built into the walls and at each exchange it is always assumed that they are said.

But the Iris Room is really the ultimate. The light comes through seven different layers of glass, and it is very dim when it arrives. And there the more daring remove their goggles entirely and go about without them in the multi-colored twilight. This is illegal. It is even foolhardy. There is no earthly equivalent to it. To divest oneself and disport with Nudist would be tame by comparison. But Mitzi and her friends were of the reckless generation, and the Iris Room was their rendezvous.

The orgy will not be detailed here. The floor show was wild. Yet we cannot credit the rumor that the comedian was so crude as to look directly at the audience even in that colored twilight; or they so gauche as to laugh outright at the jokes, they who had been taught always to murmur. "One knows of one who knows of one who ventures to smile." Yet there was no doubting that the Iris Room was a lively place. And when they left it at dawn, Marlow was pleased and sleepy and tipsy.

There was a week of pleasure on Pudibundia: swimming with Mitzi down at West Beach, gourmandizing with Mitzi at Gastrophiles, dancing with Mitzi, pub-crawling, romancing, carrying on generally. The money exchange was favorable and Marlow was on an expense account. It was a delightful time.

But still he did not forget the job he was on, and in the midst of his pleasure he sought always for information.

"When I return here," he said slyly, "we will do the many things that time does not allow. When I come back here—"

"But you will not return," said Mitzi. "Nobody ever does."

"And why not? It is surely a pleasant place to return to. Why won't I return?"

"If you cannot guess, then I cannot tell you. Do you have to know why?"

"Yes, I have to know why. That is why I came here, to find out. To find out why the young men who come here will never be able to return here, or to anywhere else."

"I can't tell you."

"Then give me a clue."

"In the Iris Room was a clue. It was not till the colour-filtered light intruded between us that we might safely take off our goggles. I would save you if I could. I want you to come back. But those higher in authority make the decisions. When you leave you will not return here, or anywhere else. But already one has spoken to one who has spoken to one who has spoken too much."

"There is a point beyond which politeness is no longer a virtue, Mitzi."

"I know. If I could change it, I would."

* * * *

So the period of the visit was at an end, and Marlow was at his last conference with OMTLM, following which he would leave Pudibundia, perhaps forever.

"Is there anything at all else you would like to know?" asked OMTLM.

"There is almost *everything* that I still want to know. I have found out nothing."

"Then ask."

"I don't know how. If I knew the questions to ask, it is possible that I would already know the answers."

"Yes, that is entirely possible."

OMTLM seemed to look at him with amused eyes. And yet the eyes were hidden behind purple goggles. Marlow had never seen the eyes of OMTLM. He had never seen the eyes of any of the Puds. Even in the Iris Room, in that strangely colored light, it had not been possible to see their eyes.

"Are you compelling me to do something?" asked Marlow.

"I may be compelling you to think of the question that has eluded you."

"Would you swear that I have not been given some fatal sickness?"

"I can swear that to the very best of my knowledge you have not."

"Are you laughing at me with your eyes?"

"No. My eyes have compassion for you."

"I have to see them."

"You are asking that?"

"Yes. I believe the answer to my question is there," Marlow said firmly.

OMTLM took off his purple goggles. His were clear, intelligent eyes and there was genuine compassion in them.

"Thank you," said Marlow. "If the answer is there, it still eludes me. I have failed in my mission for information. But I will return again. I will still find out what it is that is wrong here."

"No. You will not return."

"What will prevent me?" asked Marlow.

"Your death in a very few weeks."

"What will I die of?"

"What did all your young pilots die of?"

"But you swore that you did not know of any sickness I could have caught here!" Marlow cried.

"That was true when I said it. It was not true a moment later."

"Did all the pilots ask to see your eyes?"

"Yes. All. Curiosity is a failing of you Earthlings."

"Is it that the direct gaze of the Puds kills?"

"Yes. Even ourselves it would kill. That is why we have our eyes always shielded. That is also why we erect another shield: that of our ritual politeness, so that we may never forget that too intimate an encounter of our persons may be fatal."

"Then you have just murdered me?"

"Let us say rather that one hears of one who hears of one who killed unwillingly."

"Why did you do it to me?" demanded Marlow.

"You asked to see my eyes. It would not be polite to refuse."

"It takes you several weeks to kill. I can do it in a few seconds."

"You would be wrong to try. Our second glance kills instantly."

"Let's see if it's faster than a gun!"

* * * *

But OMTLM had not lied. It is not polite to lie on Pudibundia.

Marlow died instantly.

And that is why (though you might sometimes hear a young pilot tell amusing stories immediately—oh, very immediately—on his return from Pudibundia) you will never find an old pilot who has ever been there.

IN THE GARDEN

The protozoic recorder chirped like a bird. Not only would there be life traces on that little moon, but it would be a lively place. So they skipped several steps in the procedure.

The chordata discerner read *Positive* over most of the surface. There was spinal fluid on that orb, rivers of it. So again they omitted several tests and went to the cognition scanner. Would it show Thought on the body?

Naturally they did not get results at once, nor did they expect to; it required a fine adjustment. But they were disappointed that they found nothing for several hours as they hovered high over the rotation. Then it came, clearly and definitely, but from quite a small location only.

"Limited," said Steiner, "as though within a pale. As follow the rest of the surface to find another, or concentrate though there were but one city, if that is its form. Shall we on this? It'll be twelve hours before it's back in our ken if we let it go now."

"Let's lock on this one and finish the scan. Then we can do the rest of the world to make sure we've missed nothing," said Stark.

There was one more test to run, one very tricky and difficult of analysis, that of the Extraordinary Perception Locator. This was designed simply to locate a source of superior thought. But this might be so varied or so unfamiliar that often both the machine and the designer of it were puzzled as how to read the results.

The E. P. Locator had been designed by Glaser. But when the Locator had refused to read *Positive* when turned on the inventor himself, bad blood developed between machine and man. Glaser knew that he had extraordinary perception. He was a much honored man in his field. He told the machine so heatedly.

The machine replied, with such warmth that its relays chattered, that Glaser did *not* have extraordinary perception; he had only ordinary perception to an extraordinary degree. There is a *difference*, the machine insisted.

It was for this reason that Glaser used that model no more, but built others more amenable. And it was for this reason also that the owners of Little Probe had acquired the original machine so cheaply.

And there was no denying that the Extraordinary Perception Locator (or Eppel) was a contrary machine. On Earth it had read *Positive* on a number of crack-pots, including Waxey Sax, a jazz tootler who could not even read music. But it had also read *Positive* on ninety percent of the acknowledged superior minds of the Earth. In space it had been a sound guide to the unusual intelligences encountered. Yet on Suzuki-Mi it had read *Positive* on a two-inch long worm, one only out of billions. For the countless identical worms no trace of anything at all was shown by the test.

So it was with mixed emotions that Steiner locked onto the area and got a flick. He then narrowed to a smaller area (apparently one individual, though this could not be certain) and got very definite action. Eppel was busy. The machine had a touch of the ham in it, and assumed an air of importance when it ran these tests.

Finally it signaled the result, the most exasperating result it ever produces: the single orange light. It was the equivalent of the shrug of the shoulders in a man. They called it the "You tell *me* light."

So among the intelligences on that body there was at least one that might be extraordinary, though possibly in a crack-pot way. It is good to be forewarned.

"Scan the remainder of the world, Steiner," said Stark, "and the rest of us will get some sleep. If you find no other spot then we will go down on that one the next time it is in position under us, in about twelve hours."

"You don't want to visit any of the other areas first? Somewhere away from the thoughtful creature?"

"No. The rest of the world may be dangerous. There must be a reason that Thought is in one spot only. If we find no others then we will go down boldly and visit this."

So they all, except Steiner, went off to their bunks then: Stark, the captain; Caspar Craig, supercargo, tycoon and fifty-one percent owner of the Little Probe; Gregory Gilbert, the executive officer; and F. R. Briton, S. J., a Jesuit priest who was linguist and checker champion of the craft.

Dawn did not come to the moon-town. The Little Probe hovered stationary in the light and the moon-town came up under the dawn. Then the Probe went down to visit whatever was there.

"There's no town," said Steiner. "Not a building. Yet we're on the track of the minds. There's nothing but a meadow and some boscage, a sort of fountain or pool, and four streams booming out of it."

"Keep on toward the minds," said Stark. "They're our target."

"Not a building, not two sticks or stones placed together. It looks like an Earth-type sheep there. And that looks like an Earth-lion, I'm almost afraid to say it. And those two—why they could be Earth-people. But with a difference. Where is that bright light coming from?"

"I don't know, but they're right in the middle of it. Land here. We'll go to meet them at once. Timidity has never been an efficacious tool with us."

Well, they were people. And one could only wish that all people were like them. There was a man and a woman, and they were clothed either in very bright garments or no garments at all, but only in a very bright light.

"Talk to them, Father Briton," said Stark. "You are the linguist."

"Howdy," said the priest.

He may or may not have been understood, but the two of them smiled at him so he went on.

"Father Briton from Philadelphia," he said, "on detached service. And you, my good man, what is your handle, your monicker, your tag?"

"Ha-Adamah," said the man.

"And your daughter, or niece?"

It may be that the shining man frowned momentarily at this; but the woman smiled, proving that she was human.

"The woman is named Hawwah," said the man. "The sheep is named sheep, the lion is named lion, the horse is named horse, and the hoolock is named hoolock."

"I understand. It is possible that this could go on and on. How is it that you use the English tongue?"

"I have only one tongue; but it is given to us to be understood by all; by the eagle, by the squirrel, by the ass, by the English."

"We happen to be bloody Yankees, but we use a borrowed tongue. You wouldn't have a drink on you for a tubful of thirsty travelers, would you?"

"The fountain."

"Ah—I see."

But the crew all drank of the fountain to be sociable. It was water, but water that excelled, cool and with all its original bubbles like the first water ever made.

"What do you make of them?" asked Stark.

"Human," said Steiner. "It may even be that they are a little more than human. I don't understand that light that surrounds them. And they seem to be clothed, as it were, in dignity."

"And very little else," said Father Briton, "though that light trick does serve a purpose. But I'm not sure they'd pass in Philadelphia."

"Talk to them again," said Stark. "You're the linguist."

"That isn't necessary here, Captain. Talk to them yourself."

"Are there any other people here?" Stark asked the man.

"The two of us. Man and woman."

"But are there any others?"

"How would there be any others? What other kind of people could there be than man and woman?"

"But is there more than one man or woman?"

"How could there be more than one of anything?"

The captain was a little puzzled by this, but he went on doggedly: "Ha-Adamah, what do you think that we are? Are we not people?"

"You are not anything till I name you. But I will name you and then you can be. You are named captain. He is named priest. He is named engineer. He is named flunky."

"Thanks a lot," said Steiner.

"But are we not people?" persisted Captain Stark.

"No. We are the people. There are no people but two. How could there be other people?"

"And the damnedest thing about it," muttered Steiner, "is how are we going to prove him wrong? But it does give you a small feeling."

"Can we have something to eat?" asked the captain.

"Pick from the trees," said Ha-Adamah, "and then it may be that you will want to sleep on the grass. Being not of human nature (which does not need sleep or rest), it may be that you require respite. But you are free to enjoy the garden and its fruits."

"We will," said Captain Stark.

They wandered about the place, but they were uneasy. There were the animals. The lion and lioness were enough to make one cautious, though they offered no harm. The two bears had a puzzling look, as though they wanted either to frolic with you or to mangle you.

"If there are only two people here," said Caspar Craig, "then it may be that the rest of the world is not dangerous at all. It looked fertile wherever we scanned it, though not so fertile as this central bit. And those rocks will bear examining."

"Flecked with gold, and possibly with something else," said Stark. "A very promising site."

"And everything grows here," added Stark. "Those are Earth-fruits and I never saw finer. I've tasted the grapes and plums and pears. The figs and dates are superb, the quince is as flavorsome as a quince can be, the cherries are excellent. And I never did taste such oranges. But I haven't yet tried the—" and he stopped.

"If you're thinking what I'm afraid to think," said Gilbert, "then it will be a test at least: whether we're having a pleasant dream or whether this is reality. Go ahead and eat one."

"I won't be the first to eat one. You eat."

"Ask him first. You ask him."

"Ha-Adamah, is it allowed to eat the apples?"

"Certainly. Eat. It is the finest fruit in the garden."

* * * *

"Well, the analogy breaks down there," said Stark. "I was almost beginning to believe in the thing. But, if it isn't that, then what? Father Briton, you are the linguist, but in Hebrew does not Ha-Adamah and Hawwah mean—?"

"Of course they do. You know that as well as I."

"I was never a believer. But would it be possible for the exact same proposition to maintain here as on Earth?"

"All things are possible."

And it was then that Ha-Adamah, the shining man, gave a wild cry: "No. No. Do not approach it. It is not allowed to eat of that one."

It was the pomegranate tree, and he was warning Craig away from it.

"Once more, Father," said Stark, "you should be the authority; but does not the idea that it was an apple that was forbidden go back only to a medieval painting?"

"It does. The name of the fruit is not mentioned in Genesis. In Hebrew exegesis, however, the pomegranate is usually indicated."

"I thought so. Question the man further, Father. This is too incredible."

"It is a little odd. Adam, old man, how long have you been here?"

"Forever less six days is the answer that has been given to me. I never did understand the answer, however."

"And have you gotten no older in all that time?"

"I do not understand what 'older' is. I am as I have been from the beginning."

"And do you think that you will ever die?"

"To die I do not understand. I am taught that it is a property of fallen nature to die, and that does not pertain to me or mine."

"And are you happy here?"

"Perfectly happy according to my preternatural state. But I am taught that it might be possible to lose that happiness, and then to seek it vainly through all the ages. I am taught that sickness and aging and even death could come if this happiness were ever lost. I am taught that on at least one other unfortunate world it has actually been lost."

"Do you consider yourself a knowledgeable man?"

"Yes, since I am the only man, and knowledge is natural to man. But I am further blessed. I have a preternatural intellect."

Then Stark cut in once more: "There must be some one question you could ask him, Father. Some way to settle it. I am becoming nearly convinced."

"Yes, there is a question that will settle it. Adam, old man, how about a game of checkers?"

"This is hardly the time for clowning," said Stark.

"I'm not clowning, Captain. How about it, Adam? I'll give you choice of colors and first move."

"No. It would be no contest. I have a preternatural intellect."

"Well, I beat a barber who was champion of Germantown. And I beat the champion of Morgan County, Tennessee, which is the hottest checker center on Earth. I've played against, and beaten, machines. But I never played a preternatural mind. Let's just set up the board, Adam, and have a go at it."

"No. It would be no contest. I would not like to humble you."

* * * *

They were there for three days. They were delighted with the place. It was a world with everything, and it seemed to have only two inhabitants. They went everywhere except into the big cave.

"What is there, Adam?" asked Captain Stark.

"The great serpent lives there. I would not disturb him. He has long been cranky because plans that he had for us did not materialize. But we are taught that should evil ever come to us, which it cannot if we persevere, it will come by him."

* * * *

They learned no more of the real nature of the sphere in their time there. Yet all but one of them were convinced of the reality when they left. And they talked of it as they took off.

"A crowd would laugh if told of it," said Stark, "but not many would laugh if they had actually seen the place, or them. I am not a gullible man, but I am convinced of this: this is a pristine and pure world and ours and all the others we have visited are fallen worlds. Here are the prototypes of our first parents before their fall. They are garbed in light and innocence, and they have the happiness that we have been seeking for centuries. It would be a crime if anyone disturbed that happiness."

"I too am convinced," said Steiner. "It is Paradise itself, where the lion lies down with the lamb, and where the serpent has not prevailed. It would be the darkest of crimes if we or others should play the part of the serpent, and intrude and spoil."

"I am probably the most skeptical man in the world," said Caspar Craig the tycoon, "but I do believe my eyes. I have been there and seen it. It is indeed an unspoiled Paradise; and it would be a crime calling to the wide heavens for vengeance for anyone to smirch in any way that perfection."

"So much for that. Now to business. Gilbert, take a gram: Ninety Million Square Miles of Pristine Paradise for sale or lease. Farming, Ranching, exceptional opportunities for Horticulture. Gold, Silver, Iron, Earth-Type

Fauna. Terms. Special rates for Large Settlement Parties. Write, gram, or call in person at any of our planetary offices as listed below. Ask for Brochure—Eden Acres Unlimited—"

* * * *

Down in the great cave that Old Serpent, a two-legged one among whose names was "Snake-Oil Sam," spoke to his underlings: "It'll take them fourteen days to get back with the settlers. We'll have time to overhaul the blasters. We haven't had any well-equipped settlers for six weeks. It used to be we'd hardly have time to strip and slaughter and stow before there was another batch to take care of."

"I think you'd better write me some new lines," said Adam. "I feel like a goof saying those same ones to each bunch."

"You are a goof, and therefore perfect for the part. I was in show business long enough to learn never to change a line too soon. I did change Adam and Eve to Ha-Adamah and Hawwah, and the apple to the pomegranate. People aren't becoming any smarter—but they are becoming better researched, and they insist on authenticity."

"This is still a perfect come-on here. There is something in human nature that cannot resist the idea of a Perfect Paradise. Folks will whoop and holler to their neighbors to come in droves to spoil it and mar it. It isn't greed or the desire for new land so much, though that is strong too. Mainly it is the feverish passion to befoul and poison what is unspoiled. Fortunately I am sagacious enough to take advantage of this trait. And when you start to farm a new world on a shoestring you have to acquire your equipment as you can."

He looked proudly around at the great cave with its mountains and tiers of material; heavy machinery of all sorts, titanic crates of foodstuff space-sealed; wheeled, tracked, propped, vanned, and jetted vehicles; and power packs to run a world.

He looked at the three dozen space ships stripped and stacked, and at the rather large pile of bone-meal in one corner.

"We will have to get another lion," said Eve. "Bowser is getting old, and Marie-Yvette abuses him and gnaws his toes. And we do have to have a big-maned lion to lie down with the lamb."

"I know it, Eve. The lion is a very important prop. Maybe one of the crack-pot settlers will bring a new lion."

"And can't you mix another kind of shining paint?" asked Adam. "This itches. It's hell."

"I'm working on it."

* * * *

Caspar Craig was still dictating the gram: "Amazing quality of longevity seemingly inherent in the locale. Climate Ideal. Daylight or half-light all twenty-one hours from Planet Delphina and from Sol Number Three. Pure water for all industrial purposes. Scenic and Storied. Zoning and pre-settlement restrictions to insure congenial neighbors. A completely planned globular settlement in a near arm of our own galaxy. Low taxes and liberal credit. Financing our specialty—"

"And you had better have an armed escort when you return," said Father Briton.

"Why in cosmos would we want an armed escort?"

"It's as phoney as a seven-credit note."

"You, a man of the cloth, doubt it? And us ready skeptics convinced by our senses? Why do you doubt?"

"It is only the unbelieving who believe so easily in obvious frauds. Theologically unsound, dramaturgically weak, philologically impossible, zoologically rigged, salted conspicuously with gold, and shot through with anachronisms. And moreover he was afraid to play me at checkers."

"What?"

"If I had a preternatural intellect I wouldn't be afraid of a game of checkers with anyone. Yet there was an unusual mind there somewhere; it is just that he chose not to make our acquaintance personally."

They looked at the priest thoughtfully.

"But it was Paradise in one way," said Steiner.

"How?"

"All the time we were there the woman did not speak."

ALL THE PEOPLE

Anthony Trotz went first to the politician, Mike Delado. "How many people do you know, Mr. Delado?"

"Why the question?"

"I am wondering just what amount of detail the mind can hold."

"To a degree I know many. Ten thousand well, thirty thousand by name, probably a hundred thousand by face and to shake hands with."

"And what is the limit?"

"Possibly I am the limit." The politician smiled frostily. "The only limit is time, speed of cognizance, and retention. I am told that the latter lessens with age. I am seventy, and it has not done so with me. Whom I have known I do not forget."

"And with special training could one go beyond you?"

"I doubt if one could—much. For my own training has been quite special. Nobody has been so entirely with the people as I have. I've taken five memory courses in my time, but the tricks of all of them I had already come to on my own. I am a great believer in the commonality of mankind and of near equal inherent ability. Yet there are some, say the one man in fifty, who in degree if not in kind does exceed his fellows in scope and awareness and vitality. I am that one man in fifty, and knowing people is my specialty."

"Could a man who specialized still more—and to the exclusion of other things—know a hundred thousand men well?"

"It is possible. Dimly."

"A quarter of a million?"

"I think not. He might learn that many faces and names, but he would not know the men."

Anthony went next to the philosopher, Gabriel Mindel. "Mr. Mindel, how many people do you know?"

"How know? *Per se*? A *se*? Or *In se*? *Per suam essentiam*, perhaps? Or do you mean *ab alio*? Or to know as *hoc aliquid*? There is a fine difference there. Or do you possibly mean to know *in subsiantia prima*, or in the sense of comprehensive *noumena*?"

"Somewhere between the latter two. How many persons do you know by name, face, and with a degree of intimacy?"

"I have learned over the years the names of some of my colleagues, possibly a dozen of them. I am now sound on my wife's name, and I seldom stumble over the names of my offspring—never more than momentarily. But you may have come to the wrong man for... whatever you have come for. I am notoriously poor at names, faces, and persons. I have even been described (*vox faucibus haesit*) as absentminded."

"Yes, you do have the reputation. But perhaps I have not come to the wrong man in seeking the theory of the thing. What is it that limits the comprehensive capacity of the mind of man? What will it hold? What restricts?"

"The body."

"How is that?"

"The brain, I should say, the material tie. The mind is limited by the brain. It is skull-bound. It can accumulate no more than its cranial capacity, though not one-tenth of that is ordinarily used. An unbodied mind would (in esoteric theory) be unlimited."

"And how in practical theory?"

"If it is practical, a *pragma*, it is a thing and not a theory."

"Then we can have no experience with the unbodied mind, or the possibility of it?"

"We have not discovered any area of contact, but we may entertain the possibility of it. There is no paradox here. One may rationally consider the irrational."

Anthony went next to see the priest.

"How many people do you know?" he asked him.

"I know them all."

"That has to be doubted," said Anthony after a moment.

"I've had twenty different stations. And when you hear five thousand confessions a year for forty years, you by no means know all about people, but you do know all people."

"I do not mean types. I mean persons.

"Oh, I know a dozen or so well, a few thousands somewhat less."

"Would it be possible to know a hundred thousand people, a half million?"

"A mentalist might know that many to recognize; I don't know the limit. But darkened man has a limit set; on everything."

"Could a somehow emancipated man know more?"

"The only emancipated man is the corporally dead man. And the dead man, if he attains the beatific vision, knows all other persons who have ever been since time began."

"All the billions?"

"All."

"With the same brain?"

"No. But with the same mind."

"Then wouldn't even a believer have to admit that the mind which we have now is only a token mind? Would not any connection it would have with a completely comprehensive mind be very tenuous? Would we really be the same person if so changed? It is like saying a bucket would hold the ocean if it were fulfilled, which only means filled full. How could it be the same mind?"

"I don't know."

Anthony went to see the psychologist.

"How many people do you know, Dr. Shirm?"

"I could be crabby and say that I know as many as want to; but it wouldn't be the truth. I rather like people, which is odd in my profession. What is it that you really want to know?"

"How many people can one man know?"

"It doesn't matter very much. People mostly overestimate the number of their acquaintances. What is it that you are trying to ask me?"

"Could one man know everyone?"

"Naturally not. But unnaturally he might seem to. There is a delusion to this effect accompanied by euphoria, and it is called—"

"I don't want to know what it is called. Why do specialists use Latin and Greek?"

"One part hokum, and two parts need; there simply not being enough letters in the alphabet of exposition without them. It is as difficult to name concepts as children, and we search our brains as a new mother does. It will not do to call two children or two concepts by the same name."

"Thank you. I doubt that this is delusion, and it is not accompanied by euphoria."

Anthony had a reason for questioning the four men since (as a new thing that had come to him) he knew everybody. He knew everyone in Salt Lake City, where he had never been. He knew everybody in Jebel Shah, where the town is a little amphitheater around the harbor, and in Batangas and Weilmi. He knew the loungers around the end of the Galata bridge in Istanbul, and the porters in Kuala Lumpur. He knew the tobacco traders in Plovdiv, and the cork cutters of Portugal. He knew the dock workermen in Djibouti, and the glove makers in Prague. He knew the vegetable farmers around El Centro, and the muskrat trappers of Barrataria Bay. He knew the three billion people of the world by name and face, and with a fair degree of intimacy.

"Yet I'm not a very intelligent man. I've been called a bungler. And they've had to reassign me three different times at the filter center. I've seen only a few thousands of those billions of people, and it seems unusual that I should know them all. It may be a delusion, as Dr. Shirm says, but it is a heavily detailed delusion, and it is not accompanied by euphoria. I feel like green hell just thinking of it."

He knew the cattle traders of Letterkenny Donegal; he knew the cane cutters of Oriente, and the tree climbers of Milne Bay. He knew the people who died every minute, and those who were born.

"There is no way out of it. I know *everybody* in the world. It is impossible, but it is so. And to what purpose? There aren't a handful of them I could borrow a dollar from, and I haven't a real friend in the lot. I don't know whether it came to me suddenly, but I realized it suddenly. My father was a junk dealer in Wichita, and my education is spotty. I am maladjusted, introverted, incompetent and unhappy, and I also have weak kidneys. Why should a power like this come to a man like me?"

The children in the streets hooted at him. Anthony had always had a healthy hatred for children and dogs, those twin harassers of the unfortunate and the maladjusted. Both run in packs, and both are cowardly attackers. If either of them spots a weakness he will not let it go. That Anthony's father had been a junk dealer was no reason to hoot at him. And how did the children even know about that? Did they possess some fraction of the power that had come on him lately?

But he had strolled about the town for too long. He should have been at work at the filter center. Often they were impatient with him when he wandered off from his work, and Colonel Peter Cooper was waiting for him when he came in now.

"Where have you been, Anthony?"

"Walking. I talked to four men. I mentioned no subject in the province of the filter center."

"Every subject is in the province of the filter center. And you know that our work here is confidential."

"Yes, sir, but I do not understand the import of my work here. I would not be able to give out information that I do not have."

"A popular misconception. There are others who might understand the import of it, and be able to reconstruct it from what you tell them. How do you feel?"

"Nervous, unwell, my tongue is furred, and my kidneys—"

"Ah yes, there will be someone here this afternoon to fix your kidneys. I have not forgotten. Is there anything that you want to tell me?"

"No, sir."

Colonel Cooper had the habit of asking that of his workers in the manner of a mother asking a child if he wants to go to the bathroom. There was something embarrassing in his intonation.

Well, he did want to tell him something, but he didn't know how to phrase it. He wanted to tell the colonel that he had newly acquired the power of knowing everyone in the world, that he was worried how he could hold so much in a head that was not noteworthy in its capacity. But he feared ridicule more than he feared anything and he was a tangle of fears.

But he thought he would try it a little bit on his co-workers.

"I know a man named Walter Walloroy in Galveston," he said to Adrian. "He drinks beer at the Gizmo bar, and is retired."

"What is the superlative of *so what*?"

"But I have never been there," said Anthony.

"And I have never been in Kalamazoo."

"I know a girl in Kalamazoo. Her name is Greta Harandash. She is home today with a cold. She is prone to colds."

But Adrian was a creature both uninterested and uninteresting. It is very hard to confide in one who is uninterested.

"Well, I will live with it a little while," said Anthony. "Or I may have to go to a doctor and see if he can give me something to make all these people go away. But if he thinks my story is a queer one, he may report me back to the center, and I might be reclassified again. It makes me nervous to be reclassified."

So he lived with it a while, the rest of the day and the night. He should have felt better. A man had come that afternoon and fixed his kidneys; but there was nobody to fix his nervousness and apprehension. And his skittishness was increased when the children hooted at him as he walked to work in the morning. That hated epithet! But how could they know that his father had been a dealer in used metals in a town far away?

He had to confide in someone.

He spoke to Wellington, who also worked in his room. "I know a girl in Beirut who is just going to bed. It is evening there now, you know."

"That so? Why don't they get their time straightened out? I met a girl last night that's cute as a correlator key, and kind of shaped like one. She doesn't know yet that I work in the center and am a restricted person. I'm not going to tell her. Let her find out for herself."

It was no good trying to tell things to Wellington. Wellington never listened. And then Anthony got a summons to Colonel Peter Cooper, which always increased his apprehension.

"Anthony," said the colonel, "I want you to tell me if you discern anything unusual. That is really your job, to report anything unusual. The other, the paper shuffling, is just something to keep your idle hands busy. Now tell me clearly if anything unusual has come to your notice."

"Sir, it has." And then he blurted it out. "I know everybody. I know everybody in the world. I know them all in their billions, every person. It has me worried sick."

"Yes, yes, Anthony. But tell me, have you noticed anything odd? It is your duty to tell me if you have."

"But I have just told you! In some manner I know every person in the world. I know the people in Transvaal, I know the people in Guatemala. I know everybody."

"Yes, Anthony, we realize that. And it may take a little getting used to. But that isn't what I mean. Have you, besides that thing that seems out of the way to you, noticed anything unusual, anything that seems out of place, a little bit wrong?"

"Ah, besides that and your reaction to it, no, sir. Nothing else odd. I might ask, though, how odd can a thing get? But other than that, no, sir."

"Good, Anthony. Now remember, if you sense anything odd about anything at all, come and tell me. No matter how trivial it is, if you feel that something is just a little bit out of place, then report it at once. Do you understand that?"

"Yes, sir."

But he couldn't help wondering what it might be that the Colonel would consider a little bit odd.

Anthony left the center and walked. He shouldn't have. He knew that they became impatient with him when he wandered off from his work.

"But I have to think. I have all the people in the world in my brain, and still I am not able to think. This power should have come to someone able to take advantage of it."

He went into the Plugged Nickel Bar, but the man on duty knew him for a restricted person from the filter center, and would not serve him.

He wandered disconsolately about the city. "I know the people in Omaha and those in Omsk. What queer names have the towns of the earth! I know everyone in the world, and when anyone is born or dies. And Colonel Cooper did not find it unusual. Yet I am to be on the lookout for things unusual. The question rises, would I know an odd thing if I met it?"

And then it was that something just a little bit unusual did happen, something not quite right, a small thing. But the Colonel had told him to report anything about anything, no matter how insignificant, that struck him as a little queer.

It was just that with all the people in his head, and the arrivals and departures, there was a small group that was not of the pattern. Every minute hundreds left by death and arrived by birth. And now there was a small group, seven persons; they arrived into the world, and they were not born into the world.

So Anthony went to tell Colonel Cooper that something had occurred to his mind that was a little bit odd.

But damn-the-dander-headed-two-and-four-legged devils, there were the kids and the dogs in the street again, yipping and hooting and chanting:

"Tony the tin man, Tony the tin man."

He longed for the day when he would see them fall like leaves out of his mind, and death take them.

"Tony the tin man, Tony the tin man."

How had they known that his father was a used metal dealer?

Colonel Peter Cooper was waiting for him.

"You surely took your time, Anthony. Tell me at once what it is and where. The reaction was registered, but it would take us hours to pinpoint its source without your help. Now then, explain as calmly as you can what you felt or experienced. Or, more to the point, where are they?"

"No. You will have to answer certain questions first."

"I haven't the time to waste, Anthony. Tell me at once what it is and where."

"No. There is no other way. You have to bargain with me."

"One does not bargain with restricted persons."

"Well, I will bargain till I find out just what it means that I am a restricted person."

"You really don't know? Well, we haven't time to fix that stubborn streak in you now. Quickly, just what is that you have to know?"

"I have to know what a restricted person is. I have to now why the children hoot 'Tony the tin man' at me. How can they know that my father was a junk dealer?"

"You had no father. We give to each of you a basic collection of concepts and the vocabulary to handle them, a sufficient store of memories, and a background of a distant town. That happened to be yours, but there is no connection here. The children call you Tony the Tin Man because, like all really cruel creatures, they have an instinct for the truth that can hurt; and they will never forget it."

"Then I am a tin man?"

"Well, no. Actually only seventeen percent metal. And less than a third of one percent tin. You are compounded of animal, vegetable, and mineral fiber, and there was much effort given to your manufacture and programming. Yet the taunt of the children is essentially true."

"Then, if I am Tony the Tin Man, how can I know all the people of the world in my mind?"

"You have no mind."

"In my brain then. How can all that be in one small brain?"

"Because your brain is not in your head, and it is not small. The longest way around may take the shortest time here. Come, I may as well show it to you. I've told you enough that it won't matter if you know a little more.

There are few who are taken on personally conducted sightseeing tours of their own brains. You should be grateful."

"Gratitude seems a little tardy."

They went into the barred area, down into the bowels of the main building of the center. And they looked at the brain of Anthony Trotz, a restricted person in its special meaning.

"It is the largest in the world," said Colonel Cooper.

"How large?"

"A little over twelve hundred cubic meters."

"What a brain! And it is mine?"

"You share it with others. But, yes, it is yours. You have access to its data. You are an adjunct to it, a runner for it, an appendage, inasmuch as you are anything at all."

"Colonel Cooper, how long have I been alive?"

"You are not."

"How long have I been as I am now?"

"It is three days since you were last reassigned, since you were assigned to this. At that time your nervousness and apprehensions were introduced. An apprehensive unit will be more inclined to notice details just a little out of the ordinary."

"And what is my purpose?"

They were now walking back to the office work area, and Anthony had a sad feeling at leaving his brain behind him.

"This is a filter center," said Colonel Cooper, "and your purpose is to serve as a filter, of a sort. Every person has a slight aura about him. It is a characteristic of his, and is part of his personality and purpose. And it can be detected, electrically, magnetically, even visually under special conditions. The accumulator at which we were looking (your brain) is designed to maintain contact with all the auras in the world, and to keep running and complete data on them all. It contains a multiplicity of circuits for each of its three billion and some subjects. However, as aid to its operation, it was necessary to assign several artificial consciousnesses to it. You are one of these."

Anthony looked out the window as the Colonel continued his explanation.

The dogs and the children had found a new victim in the streets below, and Anthony's heart went out to him.

"The purpose," said Colonel Cooper, "was to notice anything just a little peculiar in the auras and the persons they represent, anything at all odd in their comings and goings. Anything like what you have come here to report to me."

"Like the seven persons who recently arrived in the world, and not by way of birth?"

"Yes. We have been expecting the first of the aliens for months. We must know their area, and at once. Now tell me."

"What if they are not aliens at all? What if they are restricted persons like myself?"

"Restricted persons have no aura, are not persons, are not alive. And you would not receive knowledge of them."

"Then how do I know the other restricted persons here, Adrian and Wellington, and such?"

"You know them at first hand. You do not know them through the machine. Now tell me the area quickly. The center may be a primary target. It will take the machine hours to ravel it out. Your only purpose is to serve as an intuitive shortcut."

But Tin Man Tony did not speak. He only thought in his mind—more accurately, in his brain a hundred yards away. He thought in his fabricated consciousness:

* * * *

The area is quite near. If the Colonel were not burdened with a mind, he would be able to think more clearly. He would know that cruel children and dogs love to worry what is not human, and that all the restricted persons for this area are accounted for. He would know that they are worrying one of the aliens in the street below, and that is the area that is right for my consciousness.

I wonder if they will be better masters? He is an imposing figure, and he would be able to pass for a man. And the Colonel is right: the center is a primary target.

Why! I never knew you could kill a child just by pointing a finger at him like that! What opportunities I have missed! Enemy of my enemy, you are my friend.

* * * *

And aloud he said to the Colonel:

"I will not tell you."

"Then we'll have you apart and get it out of you mighty quick."

"How quick?"

"Ten minutes."

"Time enough," said Tony.

For he knew them now, coming in like snow. They were arriving in the world by the hundreds, and not arriving by birth.

DREAM

He was a morning type, so it was unusual that he should feel depressed in the morning. He tried to account for it, and could not.

He was a healthy man, so he ate a healthy breakfast. He was not too depressed for that. And he listened unconsciously to the dark girl with the musical voice. Often she ate at Cahill's in the mornings with her girl friend.

Grape juice, pineapple juice, orange juice, apple juice... why did people look at him suspiciously just because he took four or five sorts of juice for breakfast?

* * * *

"Agnes, it was ghastly. I was built like a sack. A sackful of skunk cabbage, I swear. And I was a green-brown color and had hair like a latrine mop. Agnes, I was sick with misery. It just isn't possible for anybody to feel so low. I can't shake it at all. And the whole world was like the underside of a log. It wasn't that, though. It wasn't just one bunch of things. It was everything. It was a world where things just weren't worth living. I can't come out of it..."

"Teresa, it was only a dream."

* * * *

Sausage, only four little links for an order. Did people think he was a glutton because he had four orders of sausage? It didn't seem like very much.

"My mother was a monster. She was a wart-hoggish animal. And yet she was still recognizable. How could my mother look like a wart hog and still look like my mother? Mama's pretty!"

"Teresa, it was only a dream. Forget it."

* * * *

The stares a man must suffer just to get a dozen pancakes on his plate! What was the matter with people who called four pancakes a tall stack? And what was odd about ordering a quarter of a pound of butter? It was better than having twenty of those little pats each on its coaster.

* * * *

"Agnes, we all of us had eyes that bugged out. And we stank! We were bloated, and all the time it rained a dirty green rain that smelled like a four-letter word. Good grief, girl! We had hair all over us where we weren't warts. And we talked like cracked crows. We had crawlers. I itch just from thinking about it. And the dirty parts of the dream I won't even tell you. I've never felt so blue in my life. I just don't know how I'll make the day through."

"Teresa, doll, how could a dream upset you so much?"

* * * *

There isn't a thing wrong with ordering three eggs sunny-side up, and three over easy, and three poached ever so soft, and six of them scrambled. What law says a man should have all of his eggs fixed alike? Nor is there anything wrong with ordering five cups of coffee. That way the girl doesn't have to keep running over with refills.

Bascomb Swicegood liked to have bacon and waffles after the egg interlude and the earlier courses. But he was nearly at the end of his breakfast when he jumped up.

"What did she say?"

He was surprised at the violence of his own voice.

"What did who say, Mr. Swicegood?"

"The girl that was just here, that just left with the other girl."

"That was Teresa, and the other girl was Agnes. Or else that was Agnes and the other girl was Teresa. It depends on which girl you mean. I don't know what either of them said."

Bascomb ran out into the street.

"Girl, the girl who said it rained dirty green all the time, what's your name?"

"My name is Teresa. You've met me four times. Every morning you look like you never saw me before."

"I'm Agnes," said Agnes.

"What did you mean it rained dirty green all the time? Tell me all about it."

"I will not, Mr. Swicegood. I was just telling a dream I had to Agnes. It isn't any of your business."

"Well, I have to hear all of it. Tell me everything you dreamed."

"I will not. It was a dirty dream. It isn't any of your business. If you weren't a friend of my Uncle Ed Kelly, I'd call a policeman for your bothering me."

"Did you have things like live rats in your stomach to digest for you? Did they—"

"Oh! How did you know? Get away from me. I will call a policeman. Mr. McCarty, this man is annoying me."

"The devil he is, Miss Ananias. Old Bascomb just doesn't have it in him any more. There's no more harm in him than a lamppost."

"Did the lampposts have hair on them, Miss Teresa? Did they pant and swell and smell green...."

"Oh! You couldn't know! You awful man!"

"I'm Agnes," said Agnes; but Teresa dragged Agnes away with her.

"What is the lamppost jag, Bascomb?" asked Officer Mossback McCarty.

"Ah—I know what it is like to be in hell, Mossback. I dreamed of it last night."

"And well you should, a man who neglects his Easter duty year after year. But the lamppost jag? If it concerns anything on my beat, I have to know about it."

"It seems that I had the same depressing dream as the young lady, identical in every detail."

* * * *

Not knowing what dreams are (and we do not know), we should not find it strange that two people might have the same dream. There may not be enough of them to go around, and most dreams are forgotten in the morning.

Bascomb Swicegood had forgotten his dismal dream. He could not account for his state of depression until he heard Teresa Ananias telling pieces of her own dream to Agnes Schoenapfel. Even then it came back to him slowly at first, but afterwards with a rush.

The oddity wasn't that two people should have the same dream, but that they should discover the coincidence, what with the thousands of people running around and most of the dreams forgotten.

Yet, if it were a coincidence, it was a multiplex one. On the night when it was first made manifest it must have been dreamed by quite a number of people in one medium-large city. There was a small piece in an afternoon paper. One doctor had five different worried patients who had had dreams of rats in their stomachs, and hair growing on the insides of their mouths. This was the first publication of the shared-dream phenomenon.

The squib did not mention the foul-green-rain background, but later investigation uncovered that this and other details were common to the dreams.

But it was a reporter named Willy Wagoner who really put the town on the map. Until he did the job, the incidents and notices had been isolated. Doctor Herome Judas had been putting together some notes on the

Green-rain Syndrome. Doctor Florenz Appian had been working up his evidence on the Surex Ventriculus Trauma, and Professor Gideon Greathouse had come to some learned conclusions on the inner meaning of warts. But it was Willy Wagoner who went to the people for it, and then gave his conclusions back to the people.

Willy said that he had interviewed a thousand people at random. (He hadn't really; he had talked to about twenty. It takes longer than you might think to interview a thousand people.) He reported that slightly more than sixty-seven percent had had a dream of the same repulsive world. He reported that more than forty-four percent had had the dream more than once, thirty two percent more than twice, twenty-seven percent more than three times. Many had had it every damned night. And many refused frostily to answer questions on the subject at all.

This was ten days after Bascomb Swicegood had heard Teresa Ananias tell her dream to Agnes.

Willy published the opinions of the three learned gentlemen above, and the theories and comments of many more. He also appended a hatful of answers he had received that were sheer levity.

But the phenomenon was not local. Wagoner's article was the first comprehensive (or at least wordy) treatment of it, but only by hours. Similar things were in other papers that very afternoon, and the next day.

It was more than a fad. Those who called it a fad fell silent after they themselves experienced the dream. The suicide index rose around the country and the world. The thing was now international. The cacophonous ditty Green Rain was on all the jukes, as was *The Wart Hog Song*. People began to loath themselves and each other. Women feared that they would give birth to monsters. There were new perversions committed in the name of the thing, and several orgiastic societies were formed with the stomach rat as a symbol. All entertainment was forgotten, and this was the only topic.

Nervous disorders took a fearful rise as people tried to stay awake to avoid the abomination, and as they slept in spite of themselves and suffered the degradation.

* * * *

It is no joke to experience the same loathsome dream all night every night. It had actually come to that. All the people were dreaming it all night every night. It had passed from being a joke to being a universal menace. Even the sudden new millionaires who rushed their cures to the market were not happy. They also suffered whenever they slept, and they knew that their cures were not cures.

There were large amounts posted for anyone who could cure the populace of the wart-hog-people dreams. There was presidential edict and dictator decree, and military teams attacked the thing as a military problem, but they were not able to subdue it.

Then one night a nervous lady heard a voice in her noisome dream. It was one of the repulsive cracked wart-hog voices. "You are not dreaming," said the voice. "This is the real world. But when you wake you will be dreaming. That barefaced world is not a world at all. It is only a dream. This is the real world." The lady awoke howling. And she had not howled before, for she was a demure lady.

Nor was she the only one who awoke howling. There were hundreds, then thousands, then millions. The voice spoke to all and engendered a doubt. Which was the real world? Almost equal time was now spent in each, for the people had come to need more sleep and most of them had arrived at spending a full twelve hours or more in the nightmarish world.

"It Could Be" was the title of a headlined article on the subject by the same Professor Greathouse mentioned above. It could be, he said, that the world on which the green rain fell incessantly was the real world. It could be that the wart-hogs were real and the people a dream. It could be that rats in the stomach were normal, and other methods of digestion were chimerical.

And then a very great man went on the air in worldwide broadcast with a speech that was a ringing call for collective sanity. It was the hour of decision, he said. The decision would be made. Things were at an exact balance, and the balance would be tipped.

"But we can decide. One way or the other, we will decide. I implore you all in the name of sanity that you decide right. One world or the other will be the world of tomorrow. One of them is real and one of them is a dream. Both are with us now, and the favor can go to either. But listen to me here: whichever one wins, the other will have always been a dream, a momentary madness soon forgotten. I urge you to the sanity which in a measure I have lost myself. Yet in our darkened dilemma I feel that we yet have a choice. Choose!"

And perhaps that was the turning point.

The mad dream disappeared as suddenly as it had appeared. The world came back to normal with an embarrassed laugh. It was all over. It had lasted from its inception six weeks.

* * * *

Bascomb Swicegood, a morning type, felt excellent this morning. He breakfasted at Cahill's, and he ordered heavily as always. And he listened with half an ear to the conversation of two girls at the table next to his.

"But I should know you," he said.

"Of course. I'm Teresa."

"I'm Agnes," said Agnes.

"Mr. Swicegood, how could you forget? It was when the dreams first came, and you overheard me telling mine to Agnes. Then you ran after us in the street because you had had the same dream, and I wanted to have you arrested. Weren't they horrible dreams? And have they ever found out what caused them?"

"They were horrible, and they have not found out. They ascribe it to group mania, which is meaningless. And now there are those who say that the dreams never came at all, and soon they will be nearly forgotten. But the horror of them! The loneliness!"

"Yes, we hadn't even pediculi to curry our body hair. We almost hadn't any body hair."

Teresa was an attractive girl. She had a cute trick of popping the smallest rat out of her mouth so it could see what was coming into her stomach. She was bulbous and beautiful. "Like a sackful of skunk cabbage," Bascomb murmured admiringly in his head, and then flushed green at his forwardness of phrase.

Teresa had protuberances upon protuberances and warts on warts, and hair all over her where she wasn't warts and bumps. "Like a latrine mop!" sighed Bascomb with true admiration. The cracked clang of Teresa's voice was music in the early morning.

All was right with the earth again. Gone the hideous nightmare world when people had stood barefaced and lonely, without bodily friends or dependents. Gone that ghastly world of the sick blue sky and the near absence of entrancing odor.

Bascomb attacked manfully his plate of prime carrion. And outside the pungent green rain fell incessantly.